The Adventures of
Mishka the Mousewere

The Adventures of
Mishka the Mousewere

by

John Dashney

Illustrated by Sheila Somerville

To Natalie & Colson:
Enjoy reading together!

John Dashney
2003

SEATTLE, WASHINGTON

1995

STORM PEAK PRESS

157 YESLER WAY, SUITE 413

SEATTLE, WASHINGTON 98104

© 1995, John Dashney

ISBN 0-9641357-2-8

Library of Congress Catalog Card Number: 95-78871

For Erin, Relissa
and Shayla

"Three very brave mouseweres, indeed!"

CONTENTS

Beginning a Diary 1

1. Into the Night 4

2. Along the Fence 14

3. Missing Mice 24

4. Sporting Chances 35

Notes from a Diary 46

5. An Instant Teenager 48

6. Icy Eyes 58

7. Hoops, Girl! 68

Notes from a Diary 79

8. A Small Secret Weapon 81

9. Clues and New Hope 92

10. Fairness, Fish and Bravery 102

Notes from a Diary 111

11. Words that Hurt 113

12. Meanwhile... Meanwhile 124

13. The Midnight Rescue 134

14. Leaving Home 145

Ending a Diary 154

Beginning a Diary

A girl chewed on the stub of a pencil, trying to think what to write. She did not like writing, but she did like chewing on pencils. Or toothpicks or popsicle sticks. Even small pieces of kindling would do if there was nothing else. Cardboard and stiff paper were okay too.

An empty toilet paper roll was just right for nibbling when she was concentrating on something very hard, like writing. The toilet paper itself was too soft — for chewing, that is — and the lead in the pencil tasted funny.

Walter said the lead was really graphite. But Walter knew many more things than she did, because he had been a human all his life.

She had been human for only three months, and full human size for less than that. Ninety days before, she had stood only five inches tall. Six months ago, she had not even been born.

Snap! The pencil broke in two. She would have to find another one and try to be more careful. Pomona Mona, her landlady, was running out of pencils, toothpicks and empty toilet paper rolls.

She opened a desk drawer and took out a new pencil and popsicle stick. Chew on the stick and write with the pencil, she reminded herself. Try to use things like humans do.

The problem was that her upper front teeth did not realize they were now in a human mouth. They would keep on growing, just like a rodent's, unless she kept gnawing things to wear them down.

She checked her teeth in the mirror by the desk and then looked at the rest of her face. People told her she was pretty, but she had trouble believing it. Her human nose was a flat little stub, and it couldn't smell nearly as well as her old one could. Her human ears were little round things that wouldn't even wriggle, and her hair covered them most of the time.

Hair! Except for eyebrows and lashes, she had none on her face. Not even any whiskers, just bare skin from the top of her forehead to the point of her chin. How could that be beautiful? Still, people said she was.

Sometimes a man grew hair on his face and called it a beard. Walter said he might try it when he gets older. When she told him she would like to grow one too, he shook his head, and Pomona Mona snorted.

"No way!" they both told her.

She sighed and looked back at the blank sheet of paper. Very carefully, she printed "The Story of My Life" at the top of the page. There! She had made a start.

But could she tell a story that no one would believe?

People weren't rodents, after all. How could they know what it was like to be born behind a crate in a basement? Had they ever lived on a diet of seeds and grasses? Did they know the feeling of cold terror that came with the sight or smell of a cat? Could they even guess at what life was like near the bottom of the food chain?

Walter and a few others shared her secret. Ivon knew. So did Officer Mulholand and Pomona Mona, and maybe Ivon's girlfriend Cindy. Rancid the cat knew too, but he couldn't talk.

She had sensed that humans were strange as soon as she became one herself. You never knew how they would react to someone different. Some humans hate others because their skin color is different, but hair color is never a cause for hate. If humans had fur all over their bodies like other animals, would that mean they wouldn't hate each other as much? Maybe she should write that down.

No. Walter said stick to facts and begin at the beginning. Okay, that part would be easy. She licked the graphite on her pencil and wrote her first two sentences.

"My name is Mishka. I used to be a mouse."

CHAPTER ONE

Into the Night

How Mishka became a human is told in *The Adventures of Walter the Weremouse*. Walter saved her from Rancid the Cat and gave her some of the old woman's enchanted cheese that transformed her from a mouse into the world's smallest human. The cheese kept her growing until it finally ran out, just as she reached the size of a normal girl.

Now she looked like a human. Most of the time she felt like a human. But learning how to act like a human, *that* was hard to do.

For three nights every four weeks — the nights when the moon was full — she was a very large mouse, not a human at all. In fact, she was the fourth largest mouse in the entire world.

Since she began life as a full-time mouse, this didn't bother her as much as it did her friend Walter. He had begun life as a full-time human. Now he was a weremouse and she was a mousewere. He transformed from boy to mouse. She transformed from mouse to girl.

She decided that being a girl was really a lot better than being a mouse. She could now see things in color, she would probably live for more than one or two years, and she no longer had to be afraid of cats.

Of course, she had to wear clothes now, and she couldn't run nearly as fast on two legs as she could on four. She also sometimes missed her whiskers and her tail.

She smiled at the thought that tonight she would have them back, even if for just a few hours. The thought made her glance at the clock on her dresser. Twenty minutes to midnight! She would have to hurry and get ready.

Mishka put away the diary, took off all her clothes, then put on a terry cloth bathrobe. She knew that in another room downstairs Walter was doing the same thing. Mishka pulled the robe tight, tied the sash, hurried down two flights of stairs and rapped on her landlady's door.

Pomona Mona opened the door. She too wore a robe, and her hair was done up in curlers. Pomona Mona's hair was *always* done up in curlers. No one knew why, and no one asked. Pomona Mona was a former roller-derby star who towered over Mishka, over Walter and even over Officer Mulholand.

"Come on in, Honey," she said. "Walter ain't here yet."

For all her toughness, Pomona Mona was a kind and trusted friend. She knew the secret that Mishka and Walter shared, and she made them both welcome in the big old rooming house that she ran. Mishka now had Walter's old room on the top floor, while Walter had moved to a bigger room downstairs.

"Somehow it don't seem right for a girl to be takin' off her clothes before she goes out on a date!" Pomona Mona said as she shook her head. "In my day, we kept 'em on!"

"But that's only if you're human," Mishka said. "Human clothes don't fit mice. I'd split all the seams and pop the buttons, and I don't like cutting holes in my underwear so my tail can stick out!"

"Yeah, I guess that would be a problem," Pomona Mona agreed.

They heard two more quick raps at the door. Pomona Mona opened it and in scurried Walter. He too wore just a bathrobe, and his feet were bare.

"Sorry I'm late," he said. "Any sign of Officer Mulholand?"

"Should be along any minute now," Pomona Mona said as she looked them both over. "You two would cause a real sensation at the Senior Prom!" she added. "Goin' to Ivon's?"

Mishka shook her head. "No, we'll go out into the woods tonight," she replied. "Walter says we can't bother Ivon and Cindy all the time, and we can't have anyone but you and them and Officer Mulholand know who we are." She winked, then added, "Besides, I think Walter likes playing King of the Forest!"

"Here's Mulholand now!" Walter said as the police cruiser pulled up in front of the house.

"Now you two keep outa trouble!" Pomona Mona warned as Walter and Mishka slipped out the front door and hurried down the steps to the waiting squad car.

"Sounds almost like our mother, doesn't she?" Walter said.

Mishka thought about it for a moment or so. "You know, I think that's what she'd like to be," she replied.

7

Officer Mulholand jumped from the cruiser and opened the front door for Walter and the rear door for Mishka. "Can't we sit back here together?" Mishka asked.

"Not if you're only wearing bathrobes," Mulholand answered. "*That's* against regulations!"

"Only while we're human," Mishka said.

"You're human now," Mulholand replied. "Where do you wanna go tonight?" he asked as they climbed in.

"Out into the country!" Walter said.

"Someplace where there are trees and fields and maybe a river," Mishka added as she made herself comfortable.

"That doesn't give me much time," Mulholand said. "Duck down outa sight and I'll hit the flashers."

Walter and Mishka ducked below window level as Mulholand spun the cruiser and headed for the highway, blue and red lights flashing. "Use the siren too!" Mishka begged.

"Not unless I have to," Mulholand answered as he picked up his radio mike. "Mulholand to headquarters," he called in, "I'm proceeding west out of town on EMD."

"EMD, 10-4," headquarters responded.

EMD stood for Extended Mouse Duty, and Officer Herbert J. Mulholand was the only policeman in the world ever assigned to it. For three nights every four weeks, he transported Walter and Mishka to a safe location where they could spend the night as mice without being discovered by humans.

People monitoring the police radio with scanners shook their heads and wondered what EMD meant, but only Mulholand and the dispatcher knew. Officer Mulholand didn't mind. After all, he had proved to headquarters that giant mice really did exist, and he was *not* over stressed and in need of counseling.

Five miles from the city the cruiser left the highway and ran down a series of smaller, bumpier roads. "The place we're going is a protected wetlands area," Mulholand explained. No hunting. No houses. No development. But keep inside the area. There's private land on three sides, and I don't know who owns it. Could be dangerous."

"We'll be careful," Mishka promised.

"And don't leave any mouse tracks!" Mulholand added. "We don't want to start any more rumors."

"What about those two human-size hitmice?" Walter asked. "The whole world knows about them now."

"The whole world knows they're locked up so tight they'll never get out!" Mulholand replied. "People think they're the only two such mice in existence, and we wanna keep 'em thinking that way! So play it cool, no sightings and no tracks!"

"What's going to happen to the two hitmice?" Mishka asked.

"Well, so far the State Justice System wants 'em. The Federal Justice System wants 'em. The medical community wants 'em for study. Seven universities want 'em for the same reason. The CIA wants 'em, but they won't say why. And there's a rumor that organized crime has a contract out on 'em. You could say they were two pretty popular mice!"

"Who do you think will win?" Mishka wondered.

"Dunno," Mulholand answered. "Everyone but the CIA and organized crime has lawyers down at the courthouse. They take turns arguing until the judge goes to sleep, then they go have lunch and argue some more. One guy wanted to give 'em new identities and put 'em in the witness protection program, provided they testify against the mob. But how do you get a mouse to testify? And how do you give 'em new identities?"

"It would be kind of difficult," Walter agreed.

The cruiser bumped to a stop. Mulholand checked his watch and shut off the lights. "Exactly two minutes to midnight," he announced.

Mishka sniffed at the night air. Already her sense of smell was sharpening. She glanced at Walter and saw that he too was sniffing and anxious for the transformation to take place.

"What do you plan to do out here?" Mulholand asked.

"Explore, swim and have ourselves a feast," Walter said.

"On what?" Mulholand wondered.

"There're all kinds of good things to eat out here, if you're a mouse," Mishka told him. "Grasses and seeds and flowers and weeds. I'd like to chew down a tree, like a beaver, though Walter says we're not supposed to." She pouted a bit at the thought.

"This is a wetland, and they're protected just like us," Walter explained.

"Don't all that stuff give you a bellyache when you become human again?" Mulholand asked.

"No," Walter said. "It seems to transform right along with us."

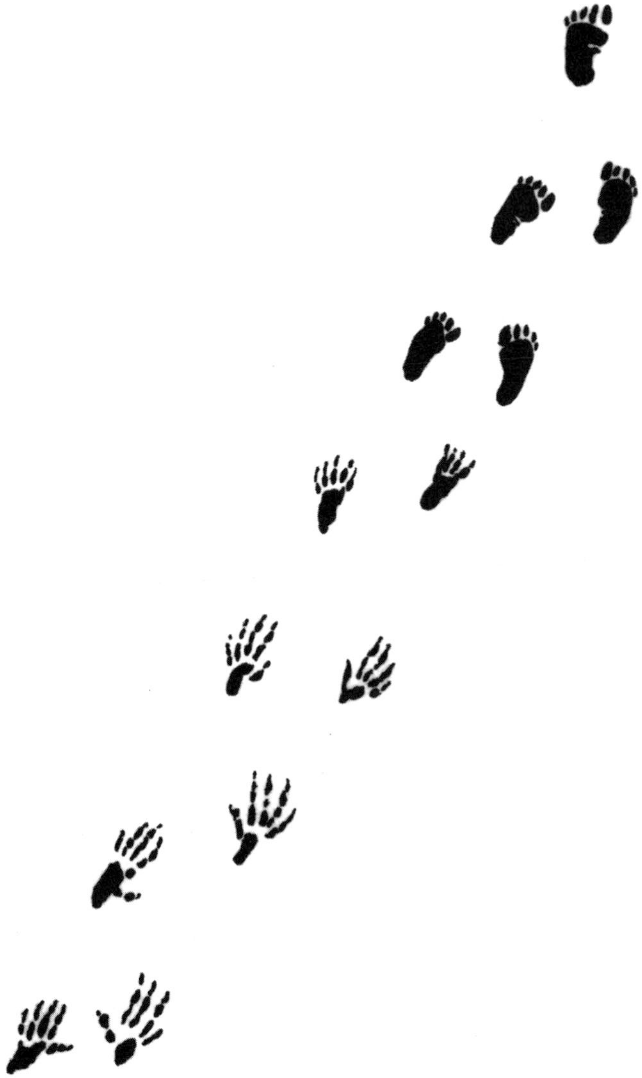

"One minute to go," Mulholand announced. He looked out at the marshy wetland and shook his head. "Anything out there you need to be afraid of?" he asked.

"I don't think so," Walter said. "There aren't any big carnivores this close to town. We'll be King and Queen of the Swamp tonight!" he added, grinning at Mishka.

Mishka still had a hard time accepting that. For most of her life she had been small and scared. Even now as a human, the sight of a hawk or owl overhead sent a shiver of terror through her. She had to stop and remind herself that she was way too big to be scared of them any longer.

She still wasn't able to hold Pomona Mona's cat on her lap either. Of course, that was okay because Rancid — as Walter called him — was too scared of her to want to sit there anyway.

If only she could be as bold a mouse as Walter, she thought. But then, maybe Walter was a little too bold.

"Thirty seconds left!" Mulholand said. "Better get ready! Eyes front, Walter!" he added as Mishka untied her robe. "You ain't allowed to stare at nekked girls in the back seat of a police car! It's against regulations!"

Mishka slipped out of the robe and crouched down on the seat as the seconds ticked off. I must be getting more human, she thought. I really don't like people staring at me when I don't have any clothes on. Yet when I'm a mouse, it doesn't bother me at all. Humans are very strange.

Walter too felt the transformation. His eyes lost their color vision, but his nose became fifty times as sharp as it had been. His whiskers sprouted and his hands became paws as he slipped them out of the robe. Suddenly, his tail was there, scrunched under him, and that hurt. He rolled over and waggled it, then felt better.

Officer Mulholand, still slightly embarrassed, got out and opened the car doors. "I'll be back right at dawn," he warned. "Be here and ready to jump in, 'cause we can't have nekked boys and girls running around a protected wetland. That's against regulations!"

Walter wondered if the Department of Environmental Quality had any regulations about weremice and mouseweres, but he could no longer speak. He just nodded and jumped from the car. Mishka did the same.

"Watch out for — ." Mulholand began, but couldn't think of anything else to warn them about. He turned the cruiser around and started back for the city. In his rearview mirror he watched Walter and Mishka race off into the night.

CHAPTER TWO

Along the Fence

Walter headed straight for a pond, while Mishka paused to sniff the night air and search for enemies. She knew it was unlikely that anything dangerous would stalk them or lie in wait. Unlikely, but not impossible.

Walter threw himself into the water with a splash that made Mishka tremble. They might as well have blown trumpets to announce their arrival. He paddled noisily across the pond, then swam back to the middle and floated silently with his legs and tail hanging down in the water.

Mishka watched him from the bank. She knew he hoped a fish or frog would swim up and rub against his tummy. Not likely! His splash probably spooked every small animal in the wetland. It was lucky they were too far north for alligators.

Learning how not to be afraid was hard. Her ancestors had lived near the bottom of the food chain for millions of generations. Predators as large as wolves and small as shrews had eaten them and their only defense had been to run and hide.

Mishka was learning to relax and be at ease as a human, but when she transformed back to a mouse, all the old animal fears resurfaced and took control. She recognized her timidity, but timid mice lived longest.

She forced herself to enter the water and swam out to where Walter lay floating like a large chunk of wood. She nudged him with her nose and tried to push him toward the bank. Mishka was hungry, and she didn't like eating alone. When they were together, one of them watched for enemies while the other fed.

Walter sensed what she wanted and allowed her to steer him to the shore. He could use a snack too, and a cattail or a water lily or some marsh grass might taste pretty good, to a mouse, that is. He was still learning what mice like to eat. It seemed to include just about everything.

So Walter and Mishka nibbled and sampled their way across the wetland. They went about two hundred yards beyond the pond and came to a fence they thought must be the boundary Mulholand had warned them about. Mishka turned back, but Walter stopped and stared at the fence.

Something was wrong.

The fence was more than ten feet high and topped with razor-sharp coils of wire. It was chain-link, like some townspeople had around their yards, though it looked far more solid than a city fence. It looked more like a prison fence, but there were no prisons out here. Why would someone have such a fence?

Was it meant to keep things in, or keep things out?

Mishka nudged Walter again. The fence meant only danger to her.

Whoever put it up didn't want them around. And when people didn't want mice around, the results were usually fatal for the mice.

Walter was still curious. A fence like this shouldn't be here in the middle of pasture and farmland. What sort of people or creatures lived on the other side? He stood on his hind legs and sniffed, but even his keen nose gave him no clues.

He looked to the left and right. The fence stretched off into the darkness in both directions. He knew it hadn't been built to guard the wetland. Someone had spent an *awful* lot of money to protect very ordinary land on the other side. Why? From whom? The answer to the second question was easy: from other humans.

Mishka's curiosity slowly overcame her fear. She crept up beside Walter and poked her nose against the fence before he could stop her. Walter was tempted to touch the fence himself, but afraid it might be electrified. Mishka had no knowledge of electric fences.

There was no flash, no sparks, no quick-fried Mishka. Walter grabbed the fence himself and pushed and pulled with all his strength. There was no give.

Let's see how far this thing goes, Walter decided silently.

He began walking along the fence line. Mishka followed. They walked on and on, but the fence seemed to have no end. Walter would've whistled if he could. An awful lot of money was being spent to protect whatever was on the other side. What could it be?

They had walked nearly half a mile when they came to the end of the wetland. The fence bent away to the left to follow a dirt road on a small hill. In the bright moonlight he saw the fence run right up the hill and over the top.

Walter left the wetland and began to follow the road, but Mishka suddenly grabbed him. For an instant, Walter was angry. Then he saw that she was up on her hind legs, sniffing the air, whiskers quivering with excitement or fright, or both.

Walter realized that he'd gone several hundred yards without bothering to check for enemies. Very unmouselike behavior! he scolded himself. He rose, sniffed and knew why Mishka was frightened.

The wind blowing toward them from beyond the fence carried the scent of humans!

Walter was aware immediately where they were: out in the open, between a fence and a road, with no trees or shrubs for cover. On the far side of the road lay a bare, plowed field. His reason screamed, "Get back into the wetland!" Mishka's instincts told her the same thing.

They whirled and sprinted for safety. How do they know we're out here, Walter asked himself. Is there a sensor in that fence? Or is this just a routine patrol? But why would anyone patrol a farm or pastureland?

Walter and Mishka ran for the pond. This time Walter eased himself into the water, barely causing a ripple. They hid in a patch of reeds near the shore, with bodies submerged and only eyes, ears and snouts above the waterline.

They saw lights bobbing slowly along the fence line, two lights that were probably two people with very powerful flashlights or lanterns. There must be a sensor in the fence, Walter thought, knowing that someone had spent a large sum of money to make sure no one got over, under or through. Why?

They heard voices more than two hundred yards from the fence, but the night was still. Their mouse ears were keen and sound carried well across the marshy wetland. So did scent. Walter could now smell two humans. They were moving slowly and carefully, as if searching for something.

"...somewheres right along here." A man's voice, low and menacing, drifted across the wetland on the wind.

"I don't see nothing," a second voice complained. "Maybe it was just a possum or something."

"No," said the first voice. "It had to be something bigger than that to set off the alarm. Something that weighed a hundred pounds or more. There's no animal out there that big."

Walter and Mishka watched the points of light dip and bob as the two guards slowly searched the fence line where they had stood a few minutes earlier. Had they left any tracks that might be spotted? Walter thought not, and certainly hoped not!

"I still don't see nothing," the second voice complained. "Ain't no sign anyone tried to go over or under that fence. Let's just go back and say it was a false alarm."

"Yes!" Mishka begged silently. "Yes! Go back!"

"No!" the first voice said as if answering her. "Something's out there! I can feel it! Radio in for the dog. We'll see if he can sniff it out!"

"I say we oughta go back!" the second voice whined. "You can come back with the dog if you want."

"And I say we stay right here until the dog comes!" the first voice replied. A light flashed out over the marsh. Walter and Mishka were too far away to be caught in the beam, but not too far away to be noticed if they moved. "If something's out there, I ain't giving it no chance to escape!"

Mishka and Walter stayed perfectly still. As long as the guards kept to the far side of the fence, they were fairly safe. The dog might catch their scent, but they hadn't actually crossed the fence. So there was no reason for the men to shoot them.

Would the men need a reason? A weremouse or mousewere is not a person. The law gives mice no protection.

A third light bobbed its way down the hill. Walter and Mishka caught the scent of a dog. Mishka knew by instinct and Walter by reason that they were downwind of the dog, so it would have a hard time picking up their scent.

Hard, but not impossible.

Walter considered swimming across the pond. Perhaps they could find a better place to hide. And even if they could not, it would still put some more distance between them and the hunters.

No, he decided. Better stay put. The moonlight is bright, and even if we manage to swim across silently, the noise might give us away when we climb out of the water.

The dog began to yip and bark, then it howled. It had picked up their scent. What would happen now?

"Something's been nosing around here, all right!" the first voice said. "Bet it's still out there too!"

"Wanna go out there after it?" a third voice asked.

"No. We got orders to stay inside the fence. But that don't mean we can't shoot at something on the outside!"

There was silence for a few moments. Then Mishka and Walter heard the first voice again. "You go up that way. I'll go down this way, and you patrol between us with the dog. Maybe it can spot something."

"They're bred for their noses, not their eyes," the third voice objected.

"Don't worry. It'll be daylight before long. If anything's out there, it'll have to move soon. And when it does..."

Walter and Mishka heard another sound, the *click-clack* of a bullet being jacked into the firing chamber of a gun. It sounded strangely loud and clear across the open marshland.

Could they hit us at this range? Walter wondered. He didn't know much about guns, but he knew that a rifle bullet could travel more than a mile. With what kind of accuracy?

Mishka's mouse instinct kept her perfectly still. As long as they weren't spotted, they were safe. She knew she could stay still for hours. But did Walter have that kind of patience? Mishka began to worry about him. She was growing more and more human in her feelings. Mice never worried about others.

The dog yipped and barked again. "Right here is *where* it was," said the handler, "but I sure can't tell ya *what* it was! Don't think it was human, though. There's some kinda track. I can't make it out."

"Told ya there was something," said the first voice. "That dog don't bark at ghosts."

"Waste of time," the second voice complained. Now that they had spread out, they were all talking loudly. Walter and Mishka could hear all three quite clearly. "Whatever it was, it's long gone by now. Let's go back and say we scared it off."

"No!" said the first voice. "It's still gotta be out there some-wheres, and we're gonna find out who or what it is! The boss likes answers. He don't like mysteries!"

"Send the dog around the fence then," said the third voice. "If it's out there, he'll find it."

"Good idea, but we'll wait for daylight," said the man with the gun. "Take him back up by the gate. As soon as it gets light enough to shoot, turn him loose!"

We are in big, big trouble, Walter realized. As long as we're mice, still and nearly submerged, we're invisible in the dark-ness. But at dawn we become human again, and the dog and the coldness of the water will quickly force us to move. When we move we'll be easy targets for a high-powered rifle. Would those men shoot people?

They would certainly shoot mice!

Walter and Mishka didn't dare move, and they didn't dare stay put either. Their only hope lay in Officer Mulholand. He had said he would return right at daybreak. If he is early, he might scare them off or at least stop them from shooting.

But if he is late....

"Be dawn in a few minutes," the first man called out. "Keep a sharp eye!"

Walter looked east. The blackness grew paler. Sunrise was just a few minutes away. Whatever was going to happen was going to happen very soon now...

"Hey!" cried the second voice. "I see lights coming up the road!"

Mishka turned her head carefully and saw the headlights. Hooray for Officer Mulholand! They had a way out, *if* they could get to him without being seen.

Walter nudged Mishka and began to swim across the pond. Mishka did not like to swim across open water, but knew she had to move quickly. They swam as low in the water as they could, just eyes, ears and snouts above the surface, barely making a ripple.

Mulholand had stopped, but he kept his lights on, and they shone directly across the pond. Walter and Mishka kept to one side of the beams. If they scrambled out in darkness, the lights might distract their trackers.

Walter's paws touched bottom. Just a few more feet!

"Hey! Look at that!" a voice cried. Mishka and Walter froze. Had they been spotted? No. They saw the revolving, flashing lights Mulholand had turned on.

Safe!

Walter scrambled from the pond and sprinted for the squad car, Mishka close behind. They wouldn't dare shoot with a police car standing by! Mulholand was out and had the doors open when they reached the cruiser. Mishka and Walter tumbled in just as the sun broke over the eastern horizon.

"Have an interesting night?" Mulholand asked as he turned the cruiser around and gunned the engine.

"As a matter of fact, we did." said a now-human Mishka as she pulled her robe around her and tied it.

CHAPTER THREE

Missing Mice

"*Tova e stranno!*" Ivon said. "That is very strange indeed! A big, high fence that surrounds empty land? It makes no sense at all! Why would anyone want to spend so much money for a fence that guards nothing?"

"No one would," Walter replied. "So the fence must guard something. But what is it?"

Walter and Ivon sat with Mishka and Cindy at a table in Ivon's *sladkarnitsa* on the following night. The bagel shop was closed. It was nearly midnight, and Mishka and Walter would soon become mice again. No one could come up with an answer to the puzzle.

"What does Mulholand think?" Cindy asked.

"He thinks it is very strange too," Mishka said. "He told us he would do some checking." She frowned for a moment and then asked, "Does that mean he's going to make some little marks with his pen?"

Walter smiled. "No. It means he'll investigate. 'Do some checking' is what we call a, a... "

"Figure of speech," Cindy said, helping him out.

"This is all very strange," Mishka said. "What are figures of speech and why do humans say things that don't mean what they're supposed to?"

"What do you mean?" Walter asked.

"Yesterday we watched a football game," Mishka replied, "and the announcer said that the ball went right through the receiver's hands. I looked at his hands, and there were no holes in them!"

"No, that just means that he dropped the ball," Walter said.

"Then why didn't he say that?" Mishka asked.

"We humans are strange," Walter admitted. "But remember, you're one of us now."

Mishka glanced at the clock. "In five minutes I won't be," she said, "and neither will you, Walter!"

"I... I think I'll be getting on home now," Cindy said. Cindy was afraid of mice, even small mice. The idea of a mouse her own size terrified her. She'd never seen Walter or Mishka in their mousy forms, and she had no plans to.

"I will walk you back," said Ivon. "Soon, I will have a car and we can drive. Walter, will you learn to drive? I think you must be old enough."

"I don't know," Walter said. "I'm an orphan and all my records were wiped out in a computer accident. I don't know who I was, who my parents were or how old I am." He frowned. "Sometimes I wish I knew, and sometimes I'm glad I don't."

"I think I must be about five or six," Mishka said.

"Honey, you don't look like any five- or six-year-old to me!" Cindy told her. "You're more like fifteen or sixteen."

"No, I mean about five or six *months*!" Mishka replied. "Last year at this time, I wasn't even born!"

"Well," Cindy said as she put on her coat, "you're the biggest, smartest five- or six-month-old I ever saw!"

Mishka went into the women's room just before midnight and took off her clothes. She looked at herself in the mirror and wondered about what Cindy had said. From baby to teenager in one jump. She would never know what it was like to be a little girl.

What is it like to lose your baby teeth? she wondered. To play with dolls, make mud pies, have a friend stay overnight, go to the circus, sit on Santa's lap, get chicken pox, be spanked? Well, she wouldn't miss the last two! But the others probably would have been fun.

When Ivon returned, Walter and Mishka were once again the third and fourth largest mice in the world. Ivon poured coffee into two soup bowls, added sugar and cream for Mishka, and set them on the floor with a plate of bagels.

"It's decaf," he told them. "The world is not yet ready for two hyper, giant mice wired on caffeine. I'm going to bed. If you see any regular mice, shoo them out. You don't have to kill them, Mishka. I realize they might be your cousins."

Mishka thought this was meant as a joke, but did not really understand what a joke was. Mice had no jokes, no humor, and no cousins. What is a cousin? Why do humans think they're important? Being human is a lot harder than Professor Bagshott's book had said it would be.

Meanwhile, Walter began to prowl. Mishka knew that he wanted to go out and explore the night, but he had promised Ivon and Officer Mulholand that he would stay inside this night. He was not happy about it.

Being inside, however, was just fine with Mishka. To her the night meant danger, even when she was big. Just walking around openly was thrilling enough for her. If she really wanted to be daring, she might stretch out and take a nap in front of the heater. No regular mouse would dare try sleeping in the open, not if it wanted to wake up again!

So it was a boring night for Walter and a fine night for Mishka. Ivon came down just before dawn and had fresh bagels and coffee ready when they transformed back to humans. Walter looked upset with the way the night had gone.

"Tonight we'll go back out into the country," he said.

"Not out by that fence!" Mishka replied.

"Why not?" Walter asked. "We'll be careful. They won't know we're there. As long as we don't touch the fence, we're okay."

"Can you be sure of that?" Mishka asked.

"You can't really be sure of anything," Walter said. "I want to see just where that fence goes. We've only seen part of it. If we can go all the way around, maybe we can solve the mystery of why it's there."

"No way!" Mishka said. "I am *not* going back there!"

Walter looked surprised. Mishka had always done what he'd asked her to. Why was she backing down now? "Don't you like adventure?" he asked.

"I don't know what adventure means," Mishka said. "Does it mean you go looking for danger? If you're a mouse, you're in danger from the minute you're born. Mice don't have to look for danger. It looks for us!"

"That's not the way humans are," Walter told her.

"Okay, when I'm human, I'll try to act like a human. But when I'm a mouse, I'll act like a mouse. You should too!"

Before Walter could reply, there was a sudden banging on the front door. Ivon unlocked it and Officer Mulholand rushed in.

"You two all right?" he asked Walter and Mishka.

"Sure we are," Walter said. "What's the matter?"

"You look stressed," Ivon said. "Better let me get you a Genuine Bulgarian Bagel and some coffee."

"No time for that," Mulholand told him. "You know them two hitmice they was holding out at the zoo, the ones that was bigger than you two? Well, they're gone! Vanished! Disappeared!"

"*Boje moi!*" Ivon exclaimed.

"How could that happen?" Walter asked. "They were locked up."

"Locks can be unlocked and doors can be opened," Mulholand said. "All I know is two things. They're gone, and they don't like you all that much!"

"Do you think they're coming after us?" Mishka asked.

"Don't know," Mulholand said. "All I know is they're gone, and the zoos are screaming, the universities are screaming, the courts are screaming, the intelligence community is screaming, the police are..." He stopped and almost blushed. "Well, we don't scream, but we're mighty upset!"

"That could make things interesting tonight," Walter said.

Later that night, when he came down to Pomona Mona's living room in his robe, Mishka was waiting with all her clothes on.

"I am not going back to that wetland," she said.

Walter started to argue. Then he shrugged. "It's a free country," he said. "I guess you don't have to go if you don't want to. But I want to go back and explore that fence, and that's what I'm going to do!"

Pomona Mona was ready to tell Walter exactly what she thought of his plans, but just then Officer Mulholand's squad car pulled up outside. "He's early," she said. "He must have some news."

Officer Mulholand did have some news, but his news was that there was no news. The two hitmice were still missing.

"How could they get out?" Pomona Mona asked.

"They had help," Mulholand said. "Remember, it was out at the zoo, not down at the jail. Can't put big mice like that in the slammer. It's against regulations. They had to put 'em in a special cage under guard. Someone slugged the guard, opened the cage and took 'em out."

"One person did all that?" Mishka asked.

"Probably more than one. I don't think them two mice wanted to go. We found a couple of hollow darts. Looks like they was shot with a tranquilizer gun."

"Then they were kidnapped? Or maybe mousenapped?" Pomona Mona asked. "Well, whoever did it is welcome to 'em!"

Mulholand nodded. "Probably organized crime," he said. "I think them two know too much. I wouldn't wanna be in them two mouses' shoes right now!"

"Mice don't wear shoes," Mishka objected.

"That's another whatayacallit," Pomona Mona explained.

"Figure of speech," Walter added.

"Strange!" Mishka said.

"I've got a strange feeling that those people out by the fence that night might have had something to do with it," Walter said. "If you could check out there..."

"Can't search private property without probable cause," Mulholand told him.

"You can't, but a mouse or two could," said Walter, grinning.

"Not this mouse!" Mishka stated. "Mulholand can take me to Ivon's or leave me here."

"Sorry, Honey," Pomona Mona said. "I can't have mice your size around the place. Gives my poor ol' cat the whimwhams somethin' awful! Why don't you both go to Ivon's?"

"Okay," said Mishka.

"No way!" said Walter.

"You two are supposed to stick together," Mulholand warned.

"We don't have to," Walter said, "and don't try to tell me it's against regulations! I won't buy it!"

"Probably isn't," Mulholand admitted, "but going out there by yourself is the worst dang-fool idea I ever heard of!"

"Maybe, and maybe not," Walter said, "but that's where I'm going. You can take me or I'll walk."

"Oh, I'll take you," Mulholand said. "Can't have mice your size running loose in the city. Not tonight! Somebody might mistake you for one of them other two and shoot you full of holes. You want to be the first mouse ever killed in a drive-by shooting?"

"Take me to Ivon's!" Mishka said with a shiver.

"Glad one of you has some brains," Mulholand said. "Let's go."

Mishka walked into the *sladkarnitsa* half an hour before midnight. Ivon and Cindy were waiting. "Where is Walter?" Ivon asked. "You two are always together."

"He's going back out to the wetland," Mishka said. "Why does he want to do it? There's danger out there! I could feel it! A mouse should know these things!"

"Ah! He is only a weremouse, not a mousewere like you," Ivon said. "Don't worry. He will be back."

"I hope so!" Mishka said the words, but she wasn't sure what they meant. Mice didn't hope or wish. It was all new and very strange to her.

"You might as well face it," Cindy said. "Walter's become an in-your-face kind of mouse."

"Walter e Mishka litseto ti?" asked a puzzled Ivon. "Walter is a mouse in your face?"

"Another figure of speech," Cindy explained to both of them. "It means that he is very bold and aggressive. Isn't there something like that in Bulgarian?"

Ivon thought a few minutes, then said, "Yes. We would call him *mnogo pechena mishka*. In English that would be a well-baked mouse."

Mishka looked even more puzzled. "Why would anyone want to bake a mouse?" she asked. "Is that another figure of speech?"

"I suppose all languages have them," Ivon said.

"You should have seen the look on Ivon's face when Mulholand asked him when we were going to tie the knot," Cindy said.

"What does that mean?" Mishka asked.

"In English it means to get married," Ivon replied. "But in Bulgarian, *da vurjem vuzela* just means to tie a knot. Our figure of speech would be *da se brakuvat*, which in English would mean to be discarded."

"No wonder humans fight all the time," Mishka said. "Nobody knows what anybody means. Everyone makes figures of speech!"

"Speaking of figures," Cindy said, "yours is going to change in a few minutes, and I want to be somewhere else when it does. Nothing personal, Mishka Honey, I just can't stand mice!"

"Cindy! Inside I'll still be me!"

"I know, and I know I shouldn't feel this way. But I do!"

That night Mishka was too restless to be frightened. She prowled around the shop and tried to sort out her new human feelings. All of a sudden, she realized she must be angry. For the first time in her life, she was mad at someone.

It was Walter, of course. Why would he do anything so... so... *unmouselike?* Looking for trouble? Mice don't look for trouble. Trouble looks for them!

And she was a bit angry with Cindy too. Why did Cindy want to be with her when she was a girl, and then want to run away when she was a mouse? Was that any way for a friend to act?

And just what was a friend, anyway? Mice don't have them.

Of course, mice have mates. Apparently, Ivon and Cindy are going to be mates. That is what getting married means. It also means being mates for life. Mice don't do that. Apparently, a lot of humans don't either. And humans are supposed to be married before they have babies, but some don't do that either.

Humans are very strange. Why do they make all these rules and then not follow them?

Mishka prowled and tried to think. Mice don't really think either. This was all very new to her.

At dawn she became a girl again and realized there would be no more transformations for another four weeks. She could try instead to be a normal person, if there is such a thing.

She had finished a cup of coffee with Ivon and was waiting for Walter and Cindy to return, when Officer Mulholand pulled up in front and jumped out of his squad car.

He was alone.

"Walter didn't come back!" he shouted as he barged through the front door. "He's disappeared! Someone or something has got him too!"

"*Boje moi!*" Ivon said once again.

CHAPTER FOUR

Sporting Chances

Mulholland shut off his headlights when the squad car turned onto the dirt road that led to the wetland. He killed the engine and eased the cruiser to a stop well short of where he'd parked two nights earlier. If anybody was watching from beyond the fence, Walter would still have a good chance of reaching the wetland undetected.

Walter slid from the car and scurried into the wetland as soon as he transformed. Mulholland thought about waiting for him or even going with him. He decided he couldn't. Aiding and abetting a weremouse was sure to be against regulations.

Walter heard the engine start again as he reached the edge of the pond. This time he eased into the water with no splash. He was alone now, and any eyes that spotted him would be unfriendly.

He swam across the pond and made his way to the fence. He didn't touch it or even come within three feet of it. He wasn't sure just how the sensor worked.

I won't take any chances, he promised himself. Then again, he knew he was taking a chance. Well, there are smart chances and stupid chances, he tried to tell himself, just like there are good choices and bad choices.

Okay, time to choose. Which way? Two nights ago, he and Mishka had gone right, out of the wetland and along a road beside a plowed field. But tonight the wind blew from the right and would carry his scent into the fenced-off land if he went that way.

I'll go left, he decided. That way all the scents will come to me. If there's anything moving, I'll know about it before it knows about me.

This time Walter remembered to stop and sniff every few seconds. He tried to sort and identify the smells of the night as they flooded into his nose.

He smelled a couple of possums back in the wetland and some rabbits on the far side of the fence. Mice too, the regular kind, and birds nesting somewhere on the ground.

At the end of the fence, he guessed he'd traveled about two hundred yards. He turned to his right and followed the fence away from the wetland. The land here was lower and marshier than up by the road.

The wind blew straight across the fence toward him, with smells from that mysterious area inside the fence. He rose on his hind legs and took a deep whiff. Mice, rabbits and birds. Somewhere a small predator, probably a weasel. Nothing to fear from that.

Suddenly, there was another scent, strange, yet somehow familiar, human and mouselike at the same time. Walter froze. It was like his own scent, and Mishka's, the smell of a were-mouse or mousewere! What was it doing out here?

It had to be that of hitmice. Walter ran a few steps, stopped and sniffed again. The scent was stronger now, one hitmouse coming his way. Where was the other?

As if in answer, a rifle shot ripped apart the stillness of the night. The report echoed, then echoed again across the wetland. Walter thought he heard another sound: the sudden, sharp cry of an animal in pain. If he had really heard it, it was only for a fraction of a second.

Something was shot, he realized. One of the hitmice? The other one was coming his way and moving fast. It was time to find a hiding place. He was no longer a hunter; he was about to be the hunted!

There were no trees on Walter's side of the fence, but patches of reeds and cattails and thick, high grass where he could hide securely. He had barely enough time to conceal himself when his night-sharp eyes spotted something coming over the crest of a small hill about three hundred yards away. It was heading straight for him with speed.

Hitmouse! His mouse-keen nose picked up another scent: dogs! He heard them yelp and howl. The hitmouse was on the run, and the dogs were right behind it!

The hitmouse ran straight for the fence and made no effort to hide or throw the dogs off the scent. When it reached the fence, barely forty yards from where Walter lay hidden, it began to dig. Walter had never seen an animal burrow so fast. The earth flew out from behind its four paws as it tunneled desperately.

Now Walter could see the dogs, two, three, four of them as they crested the hill and charged for the burrower. Could the hitmouse dig fast enough? It just might make it!

Walter realized that if the hitmouse made it under the fence, the dogs would come right under after it, and all of them would run straight to where he was hiding. Would the dogs care which giant mouse they nailed?

Probably not!

Then Walter heard a low hum. Something with a bright light topped the hill and raced for the fence even faster than the dogs. It looks and sounds like a golf cart, Walter thought. What's it doing out here?

The cart stopped. Walter heard a sharp, high-pitched noise that made him wince and cover his ears. Dog whistle, he realized, the kind that are pitched too high for human ears, but not too high for weremice!

The burrowing hitmouse was nearly under the fence when the sound made it freeze. The dogs stopped too. A man jumped from the cart and put something to his shoulder. Walter knew it was a rifle, and he knew the poor hitmouse was doomed. He felt a rush of pity for it, even though he remembered the kind of person it had been.

Walter saw the flash and heard the bullet hit before the sound of the shot reached him. The burrowing hitmouse jerked once and then was still. There was no cry, no movement, no sound but the echo of the shot repeating itself more and more faintly until it too was gone.

The man blew another note on the high-pitched whistle to recall the dogs, then got back into the cart and drove down to the fence. Walter stayed absolutely still, not daring to move.

A second light appeared at the top of the hill. Another electric cart hummed down the hillside to join the first. It stopped a few feet from the motionless hitmouse and two men got out. They were smiling, cold and hard.

"This one almost got out," one of them said. Walter recognized the voice, one of the guards from two nights ago!

"Yeah," the other voice agreed. Walter did not recognize the voice. "A few more seconds and we might have had ourselves a real problem!"

"Why bring 'em out here and give 'em a chance to run?" the first voice complained. "Why couldn't we have just whacked 'em back there at the zoo?"

"I needed information," said the man with the gun. "Besides, it's more of a challenge this way. Give 'em a sporting chance. You gotta say this for old Honky, at least I *think* this one was Honky. He tried!"

Wait a minute here, Walter thought. This guy knows who that hitmouse was! He knew it when it was human! That means he was the one who sent the hitmice after me!

"What do you wanna do with him?" the other man asked.

"We'll take 'em both back to the house," said the man who'd fired the shot. "You know how much a hide like this is worth? I know a collector who'll pay plenty."

The second man let out a harsh, grating laugh. "So old Honky and Tonk turned out to be worth something after all!" he said. "I guessed they might, because they were the only two in the world."

"No," said the first man as he put his rifle away. "I think there may be one or two more!"

Walter's mind was racing, but his body remained frozen in hiding. Who is this man and how much does he know?

"Load him on the cart and let's go," said the man who'd fired the shot. "I'll send Dee back to fill in the hole and fix the fence. Whoever thought Honky and Tonk would wind up as fashion statements?"

Walter didn't move until the men, carts and dogs had disappeared over the top of the hill. Then he crept up to the fence and looked at the hole Honky had dug. The hitmouse had nearly made it. Just a few more seconds of digging and he'd have been able to squeeze under the fence.

Just a few more seconds of digging...

The idea terrified Walter and tempted him at the same time. A few more seconds of digging and *he* could squeeze under that fence too! They won't have had time to reset the sensor, he thought. They would never know he was inside!

Could he be sure? How would he get out again?

He knew that Mishka would run the other way as fast as she could. But he was not like her. As a weremouse, the urge to explore and take chances seemed to grow.

Timid mice live longest, Mishka would argue. Honky had not been timid, and now Honky was dead.

Walter told himself that he would be careful. I'll just slip in and have a quick look around. Maybe I can spot something that'll give Mulholand probable cause to search the place.

Maybe...

Walter was digging almost before he realized it. He was smaller than Honky or Tonk, so it took only a few quick swipes with his powerful paws to make the hole large enough to slip through. Walter took a deep breath, then wriggled through the hole and into enemy territory.

He paused to sniff. The scents of men, dogs and the unlucky hitmouse hung in the air, but were fading. He was safe enough for the moment. Should he follow their tracks or strike out in a new direction? Better follow, he decided. Keep the wind blowing toward me. Less likely to be surprised that way.

Walter rose on his hind legs, sniffed again for luck, then set off on the trail of the two men and their dogs.

There was very little cover. He didn't like that. The grounds were carefully tended, like a park, and only a few trees and bushes provided shelter. The moon was shining and Walter knew he would be very easy to spot out in the open.

He zigzagged from tree to tree and bush to bush, always with his snout in the air to detect danger. He stayed downwind. All the trees and bushes reeked of the scent the dogs had left.

Walter could distinguish five, possibly six, different dogs. The owner could have a whole pack running loose. Where are they now? he asked himself.

He thought about the time, looked at the moon and tried to figure by its position how much time was left before dawn. There must be a way to do it, but Walter wasn't sure. When is dawn? Ivon had a clock in his shop, but Walter hadn't looked at it the night before.

Guesswork, instinct and hope were all he had to go on...

At the top of the hill he saw a house, just far enough down the other side to be invisible from the wetland and road where Mulholand had parked. The house was long, low and very modern-looking. At the same time, there was something very sinister about it.

I'd better not get too close, Walter thought.

But if I don't get close, I won't learn anything...

I'll go just a bit closer, he told himself. Maybe I'll see something or hear something or even smell something, because something's not right here. The man with the rifle knew Honky and Tonk.

Honky and Tonk had been sent to track down a mouse — Walter — that had destroyed a stash of illegal drugs! Walter reasoned that this man knew about and probably owned those drugs!

All the puzzle pieces fell into place. The owner of this property was a drug lord. Not a street pusher, but someone high up in organized crime. The man would probably kill anyone who got in his way.

Walter the Weremouse was interfering...

Walter had turned to scurry back to the fence when he saw coming up the road a car that he and Mishka had passed two nights earlier. From his perch near the top of the hill, he saw the road run along the far fence, then veer left for a couple hundred yards to a gate.

From where he crouched, Walter could see the entire fence and all the property inside it. It was probably half a mile from the road to where he'd entered the property and maybe a quarter of a mile from the house, over the hill, to the border of the wetland.

The car swung through the gate and pulled up in front of the house. Two men got out. The man who'd done the shooting came out of the house to greet them. They talked and the sound almost carried to Walter's mouse-keen ears. He couldn't quite make out the words.

Perhaps if he got a little bit closer...

Walter crept carefully down from the top of the hill. He tried to stay in the shadows, but the landscape was open and the moon very bright. The voices grew louder, and he could make out an occasional word or two.

Just a bit closer...

"Rowf!" A dog suddenly barked. Two others joined in. "Rowf! Rowf!" The men stopped talking and whirled around. Walter froze and pretended to be a shrub.

"Something's got in here! Turn 'em loose!"

Walter scrambled back over the hill and ran for the hole under the fence. He heard sounds on his right. The dogs were loose, and they had picked up his scent!

He sprinted as hard as he could, but the dogs were closing fast. He realized they had the angle and would cut him off before he could reach the escape hole. He swerved left and made for the wetland. Maybe they would follow the wrong track.

But the dogs swerved too, and were gaining on him! Walter might reach the fence, but he knew he wouldn't have time to dig his way under it before they caught him. The coils of razor-sharp wire made it impossible to climb over the top.

A tree loomed up ahead and Walter dashed for it. Dogs could *not* climb trees; he knew that much. Could a were-mouse? He would find out in the next couple of seconds!

Walter dug his claws into the bark and scrambled up. Something brushed the tip of his tail as he hauled himself onto a branch and looked down at five snarling dogs just out of reach.

Safe! But only for a moment!

He heard the cart coming and saw its light growing brighter over the hill. The dogs stopped barking and sat, waiting for their master. Walter was forced to wait as well. He could do nothing else. He couldn't run. He couldn't jump. He couldn't even climb any higher.

The man in the cart seemed to be in no hurry. He yawned, looked at his watch and lit a cigarette — waiting — but for what?

They sat for more than an hour, while the dogs lounged beneath the tree. The man looked at his watch occasionally.

He's waiting for dawn, Walter realized.

And at last the dawn came.

Walter felt the first sunbeams shoot into him. He clung to the branch as his form changed back from mouse to human. The man blew his silent whistle, and the dogs trotted back to the cart. Walter knew that Officer Mulholand was waiting on the other side of the wetland about five hundred yards away. It might as well have been five hundred miles.

The man walked over to the tree. He held something in his hand.

"I thought that might be you, Walter," he said. "I brought a robe for you. Why don't you come down? It's better than sitting naked in a tree all day."

Notes from a Diary

Walter's gone and I'm supposed to miss him. That's what Pomona Mona says. That's what Ivon and Cindy say. Officer Mulholand says so too, and he doesn't even like Walter very much. So I guess I should miss him. I just don't know *how*.

Is 'missing someone' another figure of speech? I thought missing something meant not hitting it. I never hit Walter, even when he was stubborn and stupid about going back to explore the fence.

Mice don't have all these feelings that humans do. We feel pain. We feel hunger. We feel sleepy, or hot or cold. But mice don't ever feel sad or happy.

What is happiness or sadness to a mouse?

Happiness is having something to eat and nothing around that will eat you. It's being warm and dry and safe, for the moment. Sadness would be no food, no shelter, and a predator closing in.

Mice do share one feeling with humans, and that is fear. Humans are afraid sometimes, but mice are afraid nearly all the time. Now that I'm human, I don't feel the fear as much as I used to. I want to learn other human feelings now. Maybe I'll learn to miss Walter, but will it do any good?

Walter went out, and he didn't come back. It happens to mice all the time. It happened to all my litter mates and my mother too. A trap, an owl, some poison and a cat. There are so many things that can kill a mouse.

We never miss the others because we know it's just a matter of time until our turn comes.

But that shouldn't happen to people. Humans are supposed to live a long time. No other animal hunts people for food.

So why did Walter vanish?

He was a mouse, but he had not learned to act like a mouse. Even a big mouse has enemies, and the worst one of all is man.

Ivon says that if Walter survived until dawn, he could still be alive, and I must not give up hope. But what is hope? Mice don't have it either. If I'm human now, I'm going to have to learn to hope.

Being human is very strange...

CHAPTER FIVE

An Instant Teenager

"Honey," Pomona Mona said to Mishka the next morning, "we gotta face the fact that Walter might not come back. You're gonna have to decide what you wanna do with your life."

"I want to live it," Mishka replied.

"Yeah, but how?" Pomona Mona asked. "What do you wanna do? What do you wanna be?"

"This is all very strange," Mishka said. "Mice are just mice. They aren't anything else. What can a human be?"

"Look around you," Pomona Mona urged. "Ivon is a baker. Cindy is a waitress. Mulholand is a policeman. I used to be a professional skater. You see, humans ain't *born* things. They *become* things."

"Strange!" Mishka said once again.

"You could be just about anything," Pomona Mona told her. "You're young. You're pretty. You've got talent; at least, I think you do. I know you're smart."

"So how do I become something?" Mishka asked.

"I guess you start by going to school," Pomona Mona said.

"I've heard of school," Mishka admitted. "Isn't that where they send little children like this?" She stood and put a hand against her waist to indicate size.

"That's grade school," Pomona Mona said. "You'd probably go to high school. That's for kids your own size and even bigger."

"It might be interesting," Mishka decided. "Can I go today?"

"It's not quite that easy," Pomona Mona said. "You can't just walk in. You gotta be enrolled."

"What does that mean?"

"It means filling out a whole bunch of papers and stuff. In your case, that could be kinda difficult."

"But aren't children supposed to go to school?"

"Yep."

"Then why make it so hard for them to do something they're supposed to do anyway?"

"Honey," Pomona Mona replied, "you said it yourself a lotta times. We humans are strange! Let's go down to Ivon's. Herbert and Cindy will be there by now. Maybe if all of us think about it together, we can come up with an idea."

Mulholand shook his head as Pomona Mona and Mishka walked into Ivon's *sladkarnitsa* and sat at a table in the back. It was the slack hour between breakfast and coffee break.

"No sign of Walter," Mulholand said sadly.

"I figured as much," Pomona Mona replied. "We got another problem we need to talk about."

Ivon and Cindy drifted over to join them. The bagel shop was nearly empty. "What is this new problem?" Ivon asked.

"What are we gonna do with Mishka?" Pomona Mona said. "Or maybe I should say, what is Mishka gonna do with herself?"

"Can't she do whatever she wants?" Cindy asked.

"No she can't," Ivon said. "I see what you mean. She has no identification, no papers, nothing to show who she is."

"I'm me!" Mishka objected. "Why do I need papers to show that? I already know who I am!"

"Well," said Mulholand, "you should be going to school, and a school would need to know how old you are. So you would need a birth certificate to start with."

"What does that do?" Mishka asked.

"It shows when and where you were born, so people know your age and who your parents are," Mulholand told her.

"I was born in the basement of Pomona Mona's house sometime last summer," Mishka said. "My parents were mice."

"Nobody is going to believe that!" Cindy said.

"They will if they see me after midnight during the full moon."

"No!" said Mulholand. "We've gotta keep that a secret! There's something bad happening out there. First them two former hoods disappear. Now Walter is gone. Something or someone could be after you. If only the... Wait! That's the answer!"

"What's the answer?" Pomona Mona demanded.

"The Witness Protection Program!" Mulholand said. "The FBI has it. It provides new identities for witnesses in danger of mob vengeance. I know the agent investigating the case of those two missing hitmen, rather hitmice. I'll bet he could set it up."

Ivon frowned and rubbed his mustache. "That would mean telling another person about her," he said.

"It's a risk we need to take," Mulholand answered. "With the proper identity, Mishka can move around freely and do whatever she wants, within the law, that is. Right now she's a prisoner, as sure as if she was locked up in a cage like those two hoods were."

"I see what you mean," Ivon said.

"She can't go to school. She can't get a job. She can't even use the library or learn to drive! We gotta make her a real person, and we gotta do it legally," Mulholand added.

"You mean, I'm not a real person now?" Mishka asked.

"You are, but you aren't," Mulholand told her. "You need an identity, a last name and a history people will believe. The FBI can give you that. I'll call the agent right now!"

"This is all very strange!" Mishka said once again. Mulholand headed for the phone.

The agent, a man named Phipps, came right over. Mulholand swore him to secrecy and explained the problem. Phipps nodded and tapped his briefcase thoughtfully.

"Yes," he agreed. "She could be a valuable witness, and she could be in danger. Normally, we like to relocate witnesses to another state."

"But these are the only people I know!" Mishka cried. Then she added, "Along with Walter, wherever he is."

"Very well, she can stay here," Phipps decided. "But she is going to need a complete identity makeover."

"Can I at least keep my name?" Mishka asked.

"Mishka... Mishka," Phipps mused. "It *is* a bit unusual. But with all the strange names girls have these days, it might not be too obvious. What language is it from? Russian?"

"Bulgarian!" Ivon answered proudly. "It means 'Little Mouse.' I suggested it myself, and Walter named her."

"Bulgarian, eh?" Phipps continued to tap his briefcase. "All right, that's a start. But she will need a last name and a history. Let's see what our computers come up with."

"How long will it take?" Pomona Mona asked.

"I'll be back with something tomorrow," Phipps promised. "In the meantime, keep a low profile."

"Is that another figure of speech?" Mishka asked.

Ivon smiled. "I think I know what that one means," he said. "In Bulgarian we would say, *ne se naduvaj*, which means: do not inflate yourself."

"Strange!" Mishka said.

By the following afternoon there was still no sign of Walter. Mishka felt strange, a kind of heaviness settled over her. Could it be what humans call sadness? Is this what missing someone was like? Does it get worse? Does it get better? Will it ever go away?

Being human is strange and kind of scary.

Carrying a briefcase full of notes and papers, Phipps came over to the rooming house with Officer Mulholand. "We've got it all worked out," he said. "Your new name is Mishka Malone. Sit down and I'll tell you the story of your life."

"But I already know the story of my life!" Mishka objected.

"That was your old life," said Phipps. "This is your new one. You are an orphan. Your father's name was John Malone. He was an American citizen whose grandparents came from Ireland. Your mother was Irena Marinova. She was a Bulgarian citizen John Malone met and married when he was in Europe."

"What's an orphan?" Mishka asked.

"It's a child whose parents are dead," Phipps told her.

Pomona Mona sniffed and dabbed at her eyes with a handkerchief. "Oh, you poor little thing!" she said.

"Yes. They were killed in a train wreck in Bulgaria several years ago, when they were visiting your Bulgarian grandparents who were killed in the same wreck. This was back when Bulgaria was a communist country, so all the records have been conveniently lost."

"Unlucky family!" Pomona Mona said.

"That's the best kind to have, if you need to be an orphan," Phipps observed. "You were brought up by your Grandmother Malone in West Virginia, but she died last year. You have no brothers or sisters either."

"All alone in the world!" Pomona Mona sniffed. "Oh, the poor baby! What's gonna happen to her?"

"Well, that's where you come into the picture," Phipps said with a smile. "You're a distant cousin of John Malone and her only living relative in America." He shuffled some papers. "Unless you'd rather be part of the Bulgarian side of the family, that is. I suppose we could arrange it."

"Can't speak the lingo," Pomona Mona admitted. "Far as that goes, I can't talk with no Irish brogue neither."

"You don't have to," Phipps said. "Just be yourself. All we've done is give you a cousin who is no longer alive."

Pomona Mona sobbed aloud. "Poor John is dead, and I never even got a chance to meet him!"

"But he was never even alive!" Phipps explained, not knowing whether to be amused or disturbed. He was like a... a character in a soap opera."

"I cry over them too," Pomona Mona confessed.

"But you do have a new niece," Phipps said. "Actually, she'd be a second cousin once removed. Whatever, you're her legal guardian now, as soon as you sign these papers."

The tears vanished. Pomona Mona beamed and grabbed Mishka in a bear hug. "You call me Aunt Mona, Honey!" she said. "You ain't never gonna be an orphan no more! Not while your Aunt Mona's around to look after you!"

"This is all very strange," Mishka said once again.

"By the way," Phipps added, "you are sixteen years old and your birthday is on the Fourth of July. It'll be easy to remember that way, and it's kind of fitting too."

"Wow!" said Cindy. "An instant teenager!"

"Sweet sixteen!" Pomona Mona sighed. "I remember when I was that age!" Her face became serious. "But I'm not gonna have you doin' the things I did back then!"

"What things were those?" Mishka asked.

"I'll explain when these men ain't around," Pomona Mona said. "We'll need to have some girl-to-girl talks. Maybe Cindy can help out a bit. It's been a while since I was a girl."

Cindy blushed. Ivon and Mulholand grinned, and Phipps made some more notes.

"So I was an orphan as a mouse, and now I'm an orphan as a girl," Mishka concluded.

"An instant orphan, just like the instant teenager," Phipps agreed. "But you don't have to feel sad, because John and Irena Malone never existed in the first place."

Mishka though still felt that strange heaviness that settled around her like a blanket. When she closed her eyes she could see Walter's face as he left Ivon's shop with Officer Mulholand to go out to the wetland.

He had gone out, and he had not come back...

Mishka shook her head and blinked. The strange, heavy feeling grew a little lighter, but did not go away.

Phipps cleared his throat. "Here's your birth certificate, a social security card and a school transcript to take with you when you enroll. We've decided to make you a B student to start with. That's above average, but not quite high honor roll."

"She'll do better than that!" Pomona Mona promised.

"That's up to her," said Phipps. "Her citizenship marks are excellent, no discipline problems. We've left interests and hobbies vague. You can decide what you like. Read up a bit on West Virginia before you enroll. I don't think any other students at your school come from there, but someone may be curious."

"She's been reading a lot already," Pomona Mona said. "I had to get the books for her. Now she can get her own."

"This is exciting!" Cindy said. "Looking at her now is like looking at a brand-new book and wondering what is going to happen when you open it and begin to read. Where is she going to go? What is she going to become?"

"Keep your mouth closed and your ears open as much as you can for the first few weeks," Phipps warned. "You know nothing about American teenagers and their habits. It's going to be like getting a drink of water out of a fire hose."

"Figure of speech, right?" Mishka asked. "Don't worry, I'll keep my low profile."

Phipps handed over an envelope. "Here's money for school clothes and other things. Cindy can help you buy what you need. Good luck, and be careful until we sort this all out!"

That night Mishka lay awake, thinking about what would happen when she enrolled the next day. Instant teenager! From an age of three months to sixteen years at one jump! What would the next day bring? And where is Walter?

CHAPTER SIX

Icy Eyes

"**Y**ou're probably wondering why I didn't shoot you just now," said the man with the gun. He set the rifle against the golf cart and handed Walter the robe. The rifle remained within easy reach. Besides, five very large, mean-looking dogs surrounded them. Any sudden move by Walter would probably be his last.

"I had to see if it was you," the man continued. "It might have been the late Honky or Tonk up there. If you had remained a mouse at dawn, I would have shot you. Honky and Tonk were of no value to me anymore."

"And I am?" Walter asked.

"Yes," said the man. "I need information. This is the information age, after all. Haven't you heard that?"

The voice was almost kindly, almost, but not quite. Walter took his first good look at the man. Until now he'd been far too frightened to notice his features.

Walter guessed that the man was in his fifties. He was chubby, but not quite fat, like a Santa Claus who had been working out. His face was round and full of dimples, and his hair was white. If he grew a beard, Walter thought, he would look like a Santa who went to aerobics classes.

Except for his eyes...

The man had the palest, coldest, hardest pair of blue eyes Walter had ever seen. Like blue-tinted ice, he thought, two icebergs floating on an empty ocean, quiet and deadly and without mercy.

Walter swallowed hard and decided to risk a question. "How did you know my name?" he asked.

"Honky and Tonk told me before their, er, accident. They could do a few things well, although I'm not sorry to be rid of them. I guess I have you to thank for that, Walter, since you began their downfall."

Yes, Walter thought. I did trick them into the Bagshott Room and got them to eat the enchanted cheese, and that led to their capture by Mulholand and Pomona Mona. But they wanted to kill me, and Mishka too!

At the thought of Mishka, Walter shivered. Did the man with the icy eyes know about her too?

"You're thinking, aren't you?" the man with the icy eyes said as he picked up the rifle and motioned for Walter to get in the cart. "I'd be very careful about my thoughts, if I were you." He motioned again and two of the dogs jumped into the cart behind Walter and placed their heads on top of the seat next to his.

"Nice doggies!" Walter murmured. He could hear them pant and smell their breath. Neither was nice.

"Bruno and Sledge would love to tear you to pieces," the man said, "and they will too, if I give the signal. So be very careful how you think, and even more careful how you move!"

"I'll be careful!" Walter promised.

"Good!" said the man. "We'll go back to the house. You do seem like a nice young man, or are you still a boy? No matter. I'm sure I will enjoy your company, though I'm afraid it won't be for very long."

He smiled, but there was no warmth to the smile. The eyes remained a pair of pale blue icebergs.

Three men were waiting for them when they reached the house. Walter knew them as the fence patrol. The car that had come up the road in the night was gone.

One man blew a whistle, and the dogs followed him around the house and out of sight. The other two looked at Walter like foxes eyeing a rabbit. Their eyes were not as cold as those of the man with icy eyes, but they held no friendship either.

"This is Walter," the man said as he stepped from the cart. "He is going to be my guest for a while. Treat him kindly, if you know how, but don't let him leave these grounds. Understood?"

"Yep," said one. The other nodded.

"Walter," the man continued, "we don't use real names around here. I call these two Dum and Dee, short for Tweedledum and Tweedledee. Sometimes I have trouble remembering which is which."

"I'm Dum," said one.

"I'm Dee," said the other.

"They are replacements for Honky and Tonk, and their job will be to look after you while you're here. They're not the smartest pair in the world, but they're not stupid either. They know what happened to Honky and Tonk and the role you played in that."

He smiled and again his eyes glittered like pale blue ice. "I'm sure you boys don't want to wind up like your former friends, right?" he asked.

"Ain't gonna happen," said Dum.

"No way!" said Dee.

"Any questions, Walter?" asked the man.

"Yes," Walter said, quaking inside but knowing he must not let his fear show. "What do I call you?"

The man smiled again. "Very good, Walter," he said, and again his voice was almost kindly. Almost, but not quite. "I've watched you looking at my face. You're interested in my eyes, right?"

"Yes," Walter admitted.

The man glared. The smile vanished. Walter shivered. "People say they look as cold as ice. Do you find them that way?"

"Yes," Walter said again. The effect was almost hypnotic.

"Then why don't you call me Mr. Ice?" the man suggested.

Walter forced himself to look straight into the man's eyes. I can't let him see my fear, he thought. He yawned and stretched.

"Mr. Ice, I'm hungry. Have you got anything to eat?" he asked.

The cold smile reappeared. "Walter, I'm sorry," Mr. Ice replied. "You're our guest, and we've forgotten our manners. Have the cook set another place for breakfast," he ordered Dum and Dee.

"Why feed him if we're just gonna shoot him later?" Dum asked.

Mr. Ice frowned. The eyes became even paler and colder. "I'll decide what happens and when," he said in a voice that was soft like the hiss of a snake. "Your job is to do exactly what I tell you to do. Honky and Tonk did not follow instructions. I hope you know better. Do you?"

"We do!" Dum said quickly.

"You bet!" added Dee.

They went inside. The house was long and low, all bright colors, with light wood paneling. It seemed almost cheerful. But, like the icy eyes in the kindly face, something ruined the effect.

There's no warmth here, Walter realized. No love, no real friendship. This house would feel cold no matter how high one turned up the heat.

Walter also discovered that he really was hungry. The feeling of panic and hopelessness had left him now that he knew nothing was going to happen immediately. He was safe for a little while at least. He had some time.

As the time passed, his hope grew, and with hope came hunger.

"Mrs. Grey, set another place for breakfast!" Mr. Ice called out as they went into the kitchen. His voice again was almost jolly, but not quite.

Mrs. Grey said nothing. Walter had never seen anyone with a name that fit so well. Her hair was grey. Her dress was grey. Her shoes, stockings and lipstick were grey. Even her skin had a greyish tinge. She reminded Walter of a ghost badly in need of bleach.

Walter half-expected her to prepare a grey or bland breakfast, but it actually turned out to be good. He sat at a small table across from Mr. Ice, who nibbled at dry toast and yogurt and watched Walter tackle ham and eggs and pancakes. Dum and Dee hovered in the background.

"Can't eat those things anymore," Mr. Ice said with a sigh. "Gives my insides all kinds of problems. That's what getting older does to you, Walter. Just think. You're not going to have to worry about that."

He smiled again, and Walter suddenly lost his appetite.

"Eat up!" Mr. Ice encouraged him. "We'll have our little talk when you finish. I never discuss business over a meal."

It's a test, Walter realized. He's daring me to finish eating after reminding me that he plans to shoot me. I have to show him that I'm not afraid!

It was difficult, but Walter finished breakfast.

Mr. Ice made a sign, and Dum and Dee left the room. "They're close by," Mr. Ice warned. "Don't get ideas. My first question is: are you going to become a mouse tonight?"

"No," Walter answered.

"How long then before you do?"

Walter forced himself to look straight into the iceberg eyes. He could meet their stare, but it was impossible to look into them and lie. He knows this, Walter realized. How do I fight it?

"About four weeks," he said. "It happens midnight to dawn on the nights of the full moon."

"So you are different from the late Honky and Tonk. What about the fourth mouse?" he asked suddenly and sharply.

"Fourth mouse?" Walter tried to think of a safe answer, but Mr. Ice gave him no time.

"It took a while, but we learned about the fourth mouse from my two former employees. Do you want to know how?"

Walter didn't really want to know, but he forced himself to nod.

"That's how," Mr. Ice said. "Nod the head, shake the head. We spent the whole day asking yes or no questions. They couldn't even hold a pencil. I became very frustrated. I do not like that."

"What did you learn from them?" Walter asked. He knew it was risky to ask questions, but he needed to find out how much Mr. Ice already knew. Could he identify Mishka?

"We know four mice came out of that library," Mr. Ice replied. "We've accounted for three of them. What I want to know is, where is the fourth?"

Walter looked straight into the icy eyes and forced himself to lie. "I don't know," he said. "We split up as soon as we hit the street. I don't know where she went."

Mr. Ice gave Walter an unpleasant smile. "Ah!" he said. "You have confirmed there is a fourth mouse, a female too. Is she like you? Does she only become a mouse every four weeks?"

Walter stared into the icy eyes, wavered, and then nodded.

"I suppose I could force you to tell me her name, but that wouldn't be any fun," Mr. Ice said. "I don't get to have much fun anymore. I have another four weeks to find her. Let's see if I can do it without your help. I can always persuade you to talk if I fail."

"Why do you want her?" Walter asked. "I was the one who destroyed the stash. She had nothing to do with it!"

"Very noble, Walter, but also stupid. You put me in some real difficulty for a while. That stuff has to be paid for, whether I get to sell it or not. I had a real cash flow problem for a couple of weeks."

"I'm not going to say I'm sorry," Walter replied. "I'm not. Maybe I saved someone's life. But why do you want... her?"

Walter glanced away from the hypnotic eyes. He'd nearly given away Mishka's name!

"Almost got you, didn't I?" said Mr. ice with another of his cold smiles. "I need her for two reasons. First, she knows too much. Second, you're not big enough by yourself. I need two of you."

"For what?" Walter asked.

Mr. Ice smiled his coldest. "Walter, you and your friend are going to become fashion statements," he said. "Do you know what the rarest and most valuable fur in the world happens to be?"

"A mouse?" Walter tried to bluff. "That can't be! They're as common as paper cups!"

"Small mice are," Mr. Ice agreed. "But great big mice are so rare that I can name my price. Do you know who was in that car you saw last night?"

"No," Walter said.

"It was a messenger from my boss." Mr. Ice smiled again. "Yes, Walter, I too have a boss, and I suppose even *he* has a boss. But my boss wants the ultimate status symbols: two specially made, giant mouse fur coats, for himself and his lady. Honky and Tonk together made one. You and your friend will supply the other."

"Maybe and maybe not," Walter said.

"I'm afraid there's no 'maybe' about it," Mr. Ice replied. "I too have to follow orders. My boss is very upset with you."

Walter forced himself to stare back at the icy blues. "I'd do it again if I had the chance!" he said.

"I'm sure you would," said Mr. Ice. "You're a brave young man, Walter. I'm glad I won't have to shoot you."

"You're not going to shoot me after all?" Walter asked.

"I'd *never* shoot a person," Mr. Ice explained. "I'm simply going to shoot a mouse. You will be my guest here, for as long as you are human. You won't be harmed, as long as you don't try to get away. Perhaps we'll talk some more."

"May I make a phone call?" Walter asked jokingly.

"To your friend, the one who becomes a mouse? Perhaps I could do it for you. What did you say her name was?"

"I didn't, and I won't," Walter replied.

"You're getting better," said Mr. Ice. "It's going to be a pleasure and a challenge to have you here." He made a signal and Dum and Dee reappeared.

"Take Walter to his room and see that he's comfortable," he told them. "Be careful. He seems to be smart. You may have to use your brains. I hope you have some."

"Not the nicest guy in the world to work for, is he?" Walter said as soon as they were alone.

"We don't mind," said Dum. "You're safe as long as he's mean to you. But when he starts being nice, watch out!" He pushed Walter into a room and shut the door after him.

Walter looked around. The room was large, brightly lit and well-furnished, but there was no window and no other door. He heard the sound of a key turning in the lock.

He lay down on the bed and tried to think of what to do. I have nearly four weeks, he thought. That's enough time to come up with a plan. I wonder what's happening to Mishka right now.

CHAPTER SEVEN

Hoops, Girl!

"**W**elcome to American Lit. Class, Mishka," the teacher said. His name was Mr. Guggenheim, a very short man with a big bump in his throat and a voice as deep as Ivon's. The bump — Mishka remembered it was called an Adam's apple — jiggled his bow tie up and down whenever he spoke.

"There's an empty seat next to Shawana in the second row," he said. "Here's a copy of our textbook."

Mishka took the book and sat next to a large, dark girl who looked at her with the half-warm stare of someone trying to make up her mind.

Mishka wondered, am I supposed to think of her as black? Or is it African-American or Afro-American? What do I say? It was her first attempt at making friends with a stranger, and she nearly panicked at the thought of saying something wrong. At last, she tried a smile and said, "Hi. I'm Mishka Malone."

The dark girl hesitated, then smiled back. "Shawana Brown," she said. "Hope you like it here."

"We are just starting a unit on Edgar Allen Poe," said the teacher. "Have you studied Poe already?"

"Poe? No," Mishka replied.

"No Poe? Oh, woe! Ho ho!" said a boy behind her.

"Talk low. Go slow. Get in the flow if you don't know Poe," said a second boy who was sitting behind Shawana.

"Yo, Joe! I'll show I'm a Poe pro though!" said the first boy.

"Don't go no mo'! Yo just so-so! Yo can blow and crow, but yo don't know Poe! Hello!" he added to Mishka.

"Hello yourself," she said as she turned to look at them. The first boy was very tall and pale, with bright red hair. The second was almost as tall, a little heavier, and darker than Shawana. Both looked pleased with themselves.

"These two characters," said Mr. Guggenheim, "are Sean Sullivan and Joe Washington. They both like to rap. While Joe is really pretty good at it, Sean — well — he tries."

"He always think. He always care. He always try, but he don't get there!" Joe put in.

"Horrible grammar, but a good rhythm," Mr. Guggenheim said. "I put up with them because they're smart and they get their work in on time. If you can do that, you can rap here too. If not, please don't." Mishka was fascinated by the bobbing bow tie, but tried not to stare.

"This is all very strange," she said once again. "What is rapping? I thought it meant to knock on something. Is it a figure of speech?"

"Girl, where *are* you from?" Shawana asked in disbelief.

"A very small place in West Virginia," Mishka answered. This was what Phipps and Pomona Mona had coached her to say.

"That explains it," Shawana said. "You'd better stick close to me, Girl. You're gonna need a mother hen for a few days."

Mishka nearly asked what a mother hen was, but then she figured it out. "That's another figure of speech, right?" she said.

"Hah!" said the teacher, and his Adam's apple and bow tie bobbed up and down again. "Somebody in West Virginia taught her something. Watch out, Shawana! She's smarter than she acts. Now, shall we get on with the life and work of Poe?"

"I hope I didn't say something wrong," Mishka said as she opened her textbook.

"Don't fret, Girl!" Shawana replied. "You're okay. For some reason, I think I like you."

"Then why do you call me Girl? My name is Mishka."

Shawana flashed a big grin. "Figure of speech!" she said.

Mishka smiled. Mr. Guggenheim cleared his throat, and his bow tie bobbed. The class began. Mishka kept her low profile and listened quietly to Poe's poetry. It sounded strange, but it appealed to her too. She'd never heard language used that way before.

"I like this!" she said to Shawana after the bell rang.

"Yeah," Shawana agreed. "Old Mr. Googles looks kinda funny, but he's a nice guy and a good teacher."

"I thought his name was Mr. Guggenheim," Mishka protested.

"It is. Googles is just our nickname for him. But listen, Girl. Don't ever call him that to his face!"

"Strange!" Mishka said. "Does Poe have a nickname too? What do his friends call him?"

"Girl! Poe died in 1849. Anyone who knew him is long gone. He only lived to be 40."

"That seems like a long time to me," said Mishka, who was still having trouble with the length of a human life.

"Forty is nothing, Girl!" Shawana told her. "He coulda doubled that if he hadn't messed himself up with booze and drugs. Think how much more he might have written if he'd got himself straight!"

"Messed up his head and wound up dead," Joe rapped. "C'mon, Shawana. I don't want to be late for my next class."

"Let's see your schedule, Mishka," Shawana said. "I'll meet you for lunch."

All through the morning a new thought grew in Mishka's mind. People wrote their words down, and the words lived on in books long after the writers were dead. She remembered her diary. Would somebody be reading it a hundred years from now and learning from her words what it was like to be a mousewere?

Shawana found her just before lunch and took her to the cafeteria. They sat at a table with Sean and Joe, and two more girls joined them. One was very tall, with blonde hair, and hobbled by a pair of crutches. The other was oriental and quite short, only an inch or two taller than Mishka.

"Allison Chambers and Myoko Oto, but we call 'em Acey and Mio," said Shawana. "We like to hang together."

"Uff!" Acey said as she carefully lowered herself into a chair that Sean held for her.

"What happened to your leg?" Mishka asked.

"Torn knee ligaments," Acey said. "I'll be on these things another three weeks. I'll miss the whole first half of the season."

Another good thing about being human, Mishka decided. To a human, a bad leg was a bother. To a mouse, it was a death sentence. But what was a season?

"What are you going to miss?" she asked.

"Hoops, Girl!" Shawana replied. "Why do you think blacks, whites and Asians hang out together? We all play basketball. Joe and Sean are on the boys' team, and Acey and Mio and I play for the girls."

"Oh," said Mishka, who knew nothing about the game. "Is it fun? Would you show me how to play?"

Shawana blinked in disbelief. "You mean to say you've never even been on a court?" she asked.

"No," said Mishka. "It was a *real* small place. But I'd sure like to try it."

"Can you come down to the gym right after school?" Shawana asked. "We have about twenty minutes before practice starts. But Girl, you ain't gonna learn the game in one afternoon! You gotta work at it!"

"I'll call my Aunt Mona and ask to stay," Mishka said. "I may not know the game, but I learn things fast."

Shawana blinked again and looked helplessly at the others.

Mishka found Shawana and Mio waiting for her in the gym after school. Both wore t-shirts and shorts. Shawana was bouncing a basketball.

"Listen up, Girl!" she said. "This is the ball. That is the *basket,* and the idea is to get the ball in the basket. Okay?"

"What basket?" Mishka asked. "All I see is an iron ring with a net under it."

Shawana said nothing, but Mio giggled. "That's the basket," she explained. "A long time ago it really was just a fruit basket with the bottom knocked out of it. That's why the game is still called basketball."

"Strange!" Mishka said. "How do you get the ball in there?"

"You shoot," said Shawana, "like this." She tried a shot from the top of the key. The ball hit the front rim and bounced away.

"Wouldn't it be easier if you got closer?" Mishka asked.

"Sure it would, Girl! But there are five players on the other team who are going to get in your face and try to stop you." She shot again. The ball spun around the rim and then fell out.

"Why not just jump up and drop it in?" Mishka asked.

"*Dunk* the ball?" Shawana replied. "It's ten feet up to that hoop! No girl here can jump that high. Even Joe and Sean can barely do it."

"Let me have the ball," said Mishka. "I'd like to try it."

Shawana tossed her the ball and Mishka walked over to the basket. She flexed her knees and ankles and then shot straight up. Mio and Shawana stared in disbelief as Mishka rose like a rocket. The top of her head was nearly level with the rim when she released the ball and let it drop through the hoop.

"Whoa!" Shawana exclaimed as Mishka landed lightly, caught the ball and flipped it back to her.

"So much for the notion that white girls can't jump!" Mio added. "With her on the team we can win without Acey!"

"I still don't believe it!" Shawana insisted. "Have you got springs in your shoes?"

"No springs," Mishka said. "I'll do it again, if you want." She ran back to the basket, leaped and dropped the ball through.

"Double whoa!" said Mio. "But Mishka, you don't just run with the ball. You have to dribble it like this." She demonstrated.

"That's strange!" Mishka said. "Why do you do it that way?"

"Rules," Mio explained. Mishka was beginning to see that humans had an awful lot of rules for just about everything.

"See, the defender tries to get it away from you," Mio continued as she crouched and dribbled harder. "Try to swat the ball away, without hitting my hand."

Mishka eyed Mio for a second or so. Then her hand moved so fast that no one saw it. She slapped the ball free and it skittered across the court to Shawana.

"Girl!" Shawana cried. "Do you know what you just did?"

"No," Mishka replied. "Did I do something wrong?"

"Wrong? You just stripped the ball from one of the best point guards in the league! Nobody can pick Mio's pocket like that!"

"Is that bad?" Mishka asked. She wasn't sure what picking a pocket meant. Mio didn't have pockets in her shorts anyway. Maybe it was another figure of speech.

"Bad? Girl, you're the *baddest* player I ever saw!"

"That means you're good," Mio explained.

"Oh," said Mishka. She had not realized just how fast and strong her arms and legs were, compared to a normal human's. It must be the mouse in me, she decided. Like my front teeth that keep growing unless I gnaw things to wear them down. I've got to be careful and keep a low profile!

But Shawana was already running for the door. "Miz Webber! Miz Webber!" she yelled. "You gotta come see!"

"Oh no!" Mishka said. "Please don't tell anyone about this!"

"Too late," Mio replied. "Shawana can't keep a secret any more than she can fly. You can't keep talent like that hidden. We could win the state title with you on the team!"

"But I don't want a state title!" Mishka begged. "I just want a low profile!"

Shawana burst back into the gym, towing a large, heavy-set woman who carried a clipboard. "Do it again, Mishka!" she said.

"*This* is the key to our success?" the coach asked. "Nothing personal, Honey, but you look awfully short, awfully light and awfully inexperienced!"

"That's okay," Mishka said. "I need to go home now anyway."

"*Girl!*" Shawana screamed.

"That won't work," Mio said. "It's going to come out somewhere, sometime. Better to have it be here and now."

Mishka knew this meant trouble, but she'd not yet learned how to lie. "What do you want me to do?" she asked.

"Jam it, Girl!" Shawana urged.

"She means jump up and drop it in again," Mio explained.

Mishka sighed, walked over to the basket, jumped and stuffed the ball. Ms. Webber dropped her clipboard.

"That girl has a five-foot vertical leap!" she gasped. "Even the pros only go three to four! Can she shoot from outside?"

"Dunno," Shawana said. "We haven't tried yet."

"Try her from the 3-point line," Ms. Webber told them.

Shawana quickly showed Mishka how to hold the ball and shoot. Mishka's first attempt missed everything. The second hit the backboard. The third shot bounced off the rim. The fourth one swished. So did the fifth and sixth.

"Natural shooter!" Ms. Webber marveled. "We've got us a scoring machine here!"

"She can defend too," Mio put in. "She picked me clean. Got the fastest hands I ever saw!"

Mishka shook her head. "I don't think my aunt wants me to do this," she said. "I'd better go home now."

"I'm coming with you!" the coach said.

A strangely sad Mishka trudged up the steps to the rooming house with Ms. Webber beside her. "I don't think my aunt will like this," she repeated as she opened the door.

Pomona Mona was in the hallway lacing up her rollerblades. "Hi, Honey!" she said. "Did school go..." She stopped and stared at Ms. Webber. Ms. Webber stared back.

"Pomona Mona! Is that really you?"

"Calamity Chris! What are you doing here?"

"Are you this girl's aunt?" Ms. Webber asked.

"You bet!" Pomona Mona said. "She ain't in any trouble, is she?"

"Trouble? She's the finest natural basketball talent I've ever seen! I want her on the team, but she says you wouldn't like it."

"Not like havin' Calamity Chris for a coach? Oh, Honey! How could you ever think that?"

The two women grabbed each other in a bear hug and then punched each other on the arm. "This is all very strange!" Mishka said once again.

"Chris and I used to skate against each other in the old days," Pomona Mona explained. "We knocked each other on our keesters in cities clear across the country! And now you coach basketball?" she asked in surprise.

"Yep! And I'd sure like to have your niece on my team!"

"What about my low profile?" Mishka asked softly.

"She could be all-state, even all-American!" Ms. Webber added.

"Go for it!" Pomona Mona urged. "This could be your talent, and it's a great way to learn to work with others. I wish Chris and me coulda been teammates in the old days!"

"Nobody woulda scored a point against us!" Ms. Webber agreed. "Sign these forms and she can join the team tomorrow."

That night Mishka lay awake after writing in her diary. She felt both happy and frightened. She'd found one of her talents and some new friends. But would they help her find Walter? Or would they make things worse?

After all, humans were very strange...

Notes from a Diary

Two weeks now since Walter disappeared... Everything seems so unusual. I'm learning to play a game. Mice do not play games. They eat, sleep, run, hide and hunt for food. And other animals hunt them for food. There is no time for games when you are a mouse.

Time! Humans have so much of it! They're babies for more than a year, and children for more than ten years. That would be several lifetimes for a mouse.

They don't have to worry about food either, at least, not in this country. They carry this stuff called money, which they trade for food or clothes or whatever they want. And even if they don't have money, there are places that will give them what they need.

Humans have all this extra time, and they use it to play games and make rules. All their games have rules, and so do most of the other things they do.

Humans are always making up rules about what they can and cannot do. At first I thought humans would be free to do whatever they wanted, but this is not so. I think it's because they don't have to fear other animals. They fear each other instead.

They make rules about not hurting or killing each other, then they do it anyway. If one person kills another, it's called murder, and there's punishment for it. But if an army kills thousands of people, it's called war and medals and ribbons are handed out.

Why are humans so different than mice?

The game I'm learning is full of rules too. I have to bounce the ball when I move with it. I have to stay inside lines, and I'm not supposed to shove other people out of my way. But as soon as I was told these rules, I was also told how to get around them if I wanted to.

I think humans make up rules so they can figure out ways to avoid them. They do this with something called taxes all the time.

Did Walter break a rule? He walked into danger, but why was there danger? Humans fear danger, yet they like to toy with it. Why?

Officer Mulholand says there's a good chance that Walter is still alive. I hope so (a new feeling for me). Mice never hope. Humans do. It is taking me a while to learn these things.

Shawana, Acey and Mio are all nice to me, but I still haven't told them about my real self. I don't know if they would be able to understand. They think I'm just a silly little girl from West Virginia, and they call me their secret weapon.

Another figure of speech. I keep a low profile by not jumping too high or moving too fast in practice. But tomorrow night we play a game against another school, and the coach wants me to play as hard as I can. Aunt Mona and my friends will be coming to watch.

How will the crowd react to me? Humans are very odd...

CHAPTER EIGHT

A Small Secret Weapon

"**M**alone, I'm keeping you on the bench until we really need you," Calamity Chris said in the pre-game huddle. "Turner starts at guard along with Mio."

Mishka nodded and sat on the bench with the reserves. Acey, still in street clothes and hobbled by crutches, sat beside her. Shawana, Mio and the other three starters took their places on the court. It was an away game, and most of the crowd cheered for the other team.

"Got the jitters?" Acey asked.

"I don't think so," Mishka said. This was all new and different. Mice never compete just for fun. She had practiced with the team and learned the rules. She kept her low profile and not dunked the ball in practice, but knew she was quicker and probably stronger than any girl on the court. Most players were nervous because they were afraid they would play poorly. Mishka was afraid she might do too well.

"You know what, Mishka?" Acey said. "I like you, but there's something about you that scares me sometimes. It's almost as if you're not, not really human."

She laughed at the idea. Mishka did not laugh.

Phipps was afraid something like this would happen. "The more people notice you, the more danger you're in," he had told her. "Stay on the bench and keep that low profile until you know how to behave like a human. We need you. Walter needs you."

But Calamity Chris said the team needed her. "You're our secret weapon. I'm gonna bring you off the bench and you're gonna tear that other team apart!"

Mishka hoped that was another figure of speech. The whole idea of playing and winning and losing was strange.

Even her jersey made her feel strange. It was red, like her shorts, and it had the number 13 and the name "Wildcats" on it. "Remember, Girl, you're a Cat now!" Shawana told her as they dressed in the locker room before the game.

From mouse to girl to cat. Mishka was now called the very thing she feared most.

The game began and Mishka turned her attention to the court. It was soon clear the Wildcats were not doing well. Without Acey they lacked height. Shawana — really a forward — had to play center. Mio did well, but Turner was too slow. So were the other two Wildcat starters.

The other team took advantage of that quickly. Their guards double-teamed Mio whenever the Wildcats had the ball and ran their plays past Turner when the Cats were on defense. They ran up eight quick points before Shawana finally hit a basket.

When the score reached 11-2, Calamity Chris signaled for a time out. "Didn't wanna do this so early," she said, "but we gotta do something about that big guard of theirs. Malone! Get in there and take her down a notch or two!"

"Is that another figure of speech?" Mishka asked.

"Yeah! It means your team needs you! Forget the low profile, we gotta have some points. Now go get 'em!"

A warm glow spread through Mishka and she smiled. She was *needed!* All through her human life, others had helped her. Now she could pay them back, and she would do it!

She sensed another new feeling. She guessed it was anger. The other team's guards had taunted poor Turner. Now it was payback time for them too!

Mishka peeled off her warmup jacket, reported to the scorer's table and then stepped out onto the court.

Four voices cheered as Mishka entered the game. Pomona Mona, Officer Mulholand, Ivon and Cindy had all come to watch. The rest of the crowd barely glanced at this short, unknown girl as the announcer said, "Number 13, Malone, into the game for the Wildcats."

"So what?" they all seemed to say.

They would soon think differently.

The other team brought the ball up court. Mio moved out to pressure their point guard, who passed the ball toward the big guard who easily ran past Turner.

But this time the pass never reached her.

Mishka leaped between them, swatted the ball down court and then raced after it. She caught up with it at the top of the key, took one step as she gathered it in, and jumped as she crossed the free-throw line.

Mishka soared. Her eyes were nearly level with the rim when she jammed the ball through the hoop. The crowd let out one huge gasp and then fell silent, not believing what they had just seen.

Mishka landed lightly, spun as she caught the ball, and handed it to the girl she'd been guarding. The opposing guard stepped over the endline and tried to pass the ball inbound to her teammate.

It never got there.

Mishka shot into the air and grabbed the ball again. She drove two steps toward the basket, then stopped and smiled at the girl who blocked the way.

"Jump for it!" she challenged, and then took off again.

The other girl tried. She was a good six inches taller than Mishka, but at the top of her jump, her eyes were only level with Mishka's waist, and Mishka was still going up. She jammed the ball with the left hand, caught it with the right as she came down and handed it back to her astounded opponent.

"Try again," she said.

The other team's coach was jumping up and down and screaming for a time out. "Illegal equipment!" she yelled. "She's got something hidden in her shoes!"

So Mishka had to sit down at the free-throw line, take off her shoes and socks and hand them over to the referee for inspection. Then, in case there was still any doubt, she picked up the ball, walked back to the basket, jumped and dunked it barefooted.

"That's the way to show 'em, Honey!" Pomona Mona yelled.

"Oh *wow!*" Cindy cried.

"*Boje moi!*" said Ivon. "There goes the low profile!"

"I think we've got trouble," Mulholand agreed.

A very shaken opposition brought the ball up court. This time Mishka didn't steal the ball. The opposing guards were so rattled they threw it out of bounds.

Mishka glanced at Coach Webber as Mio brought the ball back down court. Calamity Chris nodded to her and raised three fingers. That was the sign for a 3-point shot.

Mishka deliberately missed about half the time in practice to keep her low profile. But this was not practice; this was for real. She was five feet behind the 3-point line when Mio passed off to her. Mishka took one quick look at the basket and then launched the shot.

Swish!

"That's an NBA 3-pointer!" Acey gasped.

Coach Webber grinned. The score was now 11-9. Less than a minute later it was tied. The other team got the ball up court, keeping well away from Mishka, and missed badly on a shot from the corner. Shawana cleared the rebound and got the ball to Mio, who passed off to Mishka as soon as they crossed the half-court line.

This time three players moved out to guard her.

"Triple-teaming!" Acey exclaimed. "They're sure scared now!"

Calamity Chris nodded. "That leaves 'em with two to guard four. You can't get away with that. Watch!"

Mishka waited until the three almost trapped her. Then she jumped and fired a quick pass back to Mio. Mio relayed it to Shawana, who was alone under the basket. Shawana couldn't dunk the ball, but she didn't miss lay-ups either.

"Get ready to go back in, Turner," the coach said. "I think we've got 'em scared enough."

Mishka saw Turner report to the scorer and knew her time was almost up. She decided to try one more shot. As the other team passed the ball in, Mishka stole it. She leaped, spun in the air, and jammed home a reverse dunk.

Pomona Mona let loose a war whoop, but the rest of the crowd was absolutely silent. One man slipped out of the stands and ran to a telephone. A sports reporter, he had thought this was going to be another ho-hum game. Now he was jabbering into the phone.

"Get a photographer over here pronto!" he said. "I'm sitting on the story of the year!"

The Wildcats took a big lead into the locker room at half-time, even though Mishka did not go back into the game. Whenever the other team made a run, she stood up and took off her warmup jacket. Just the thought of her coming back in made the other team nervous enough to commit turnover after turnover.

Calamity Chris was going over strategy for the second half when Acey hobbled into the room. "There's a bunch of photographers out there, and it looks like a TV crew is trying to set up!" she said. "Word travels fast!"

"*Too* fast!" the coach replied. "Mishka, I'll put you in for a few minutes in the third and fourth, but I want you to be a decoy. Take the three if it's open, but don't drive and dunk. Pass it off. If they triple-team you, two teammates are wide open."

Acey and the other nine girls on the team wondered how Mishka would react. Being kept on the bench was one thing. But being sent into the game with orders not to do what you do best? How would she take that?

Mishka simply shrugged and said, "Sure." Fame meant nothing to mice. In fact, they feared it. The more a mouse was noticed, the shorter its life became.

So Mishka sat on the bench as the third quarter opened. None of the photographers were taking pictures. The TV crew was standing by. They are waiting for me, Mishka realized.

The other team made a run and got to within six points. Calamity Chris signaled to Mishka, who got up and took off her warmup jacket. "Nothing spectacular," she said. "Make them triple-team you and pass off."

"Right," Mishka said and checked into the game.

The game quickly turned into a rout. Mishka scored six more points on two shots from well behind the 3-point line, stole the ball several times, and passed off to Shawana, Mio and the others for easy scores. Calamity Chris sent her back to the locker room with a little over a minute to play. Acey hobbled along to stand guard against reporters.

Shawana exploded into the room as the game ended, grabbed Mishka up in a bear hug and danced her around the floor. "We won by 14!" she yelled. "Girl, you're the baddest guard I've ever seen! You sure you ain't just a little bit black?"

"I was kind of grey once," Mishka said.

"Good enough for me, Girl! You're a sister in my book!"

"Uh, Mishka," Acey said. "There's a whole bunch of reporters and photographers out there. They all want to see you. Have you ever been interviewed?"

"No," Mishka said. "What's that?"

"They ask you a lot of dumb questions and take your picture," Mio explained. "It all goes on the TV news tonight and into the paper tomorrow."

"I... I can't have that happen!" Mishka said. "Not yet, anyhow. I'm supposed to keep a low profile!"

"You sure picked a funny way to do it, playing the way you did tonight!" Shawana observed.

"Isn't there some way you can hide me from them?" Mishka asked. Calamity Chris looked at her strangely. "You're serious, aren't you?" she said. "Sooner or later you'll have to face them, but I'll help you tonight, for your aunt's sake. We'll try the old ball bag trick. It'll work once, but only once," she warned.

The coach grabbed a huge canvas bag and shook out the eight practice basketballs the Wildcats used during warmups. Mishka got in and Calamity Chris stuffed two of the balls back in with her.

"Just to make it look believable," she said. "Shawana, you're strong. Can you carry her out while I warn Pomona Mona?"

It all reminded Mishka of when she was a growing mouse and Walter had carried her, first in his backpack and then, when she outgrew it, in a laundry bag. Thinking of Walter brought on that heavy feeling she thought was sadness. Where is he? What has happened? Will he ever hear about how I played?

"Girl, this is a mighty odd way to treat the media!" Shawana said as she toted the bag and Mishka out of the gym. "Most girls would just about kill to get their picture in the paper."

"I can't, though. Not yet. I'll explain later," Mishka said.

"Okay. I can wait. Is your aunt a big ol' gal with her hair all up in curlers?"

"That sounds like her," Mishka said.

"Well, she's sitting in a cop car, and the cop's there too!"

"That's Officer Mulholand. He's sort of her boyfriend."

"Man, and I thought *I* had a peculiar family!" Shawana said as she dropped the bag and Mishka popped out and jumped into the police car. "Maybe growing up in West Virginia does that to you."

"Did you like the game?" Mishka asked as Mulholand hit the flashers and sped out of the lot. "Was I good enough?"

"You were maybe a little too good," Pomona Mona said. "Your name's gonna be all over the sports pages tomorrow."

"Do you think Walter might see it, if he's still alive?"

"He might," Mulholand said. "What worries me is who else might!"

CHAPTER NINE

Clues and New Hope

"Mystery Girl Leads Upset Win" ran the headline in the sports section of the next morning's newspaper. Pomona Mona beamed and cut it out to paste in a scrapbook she was starting for Mishka.

"Just like the ones I kept for myself back in the old days when I skated the circuit for the Bombers!" she said. "Years from now you'll be able to look back and remember how it all started."

"This is all very peculiar," Mishka said. "Years from now" or even "days from now" really meant nothing to a mouse, who lived hour to hour and minute to minute.

"Just listen to what they wrote!" Pomona Mona said, and began reciting the story for the third or fourth time.

"A five-foot bundle of dynamite roared off the bench and sparked the Adams Wildcats to a 57-43 win over favored Westview..."

Several miles away, a man with cold, pale eyes recited the same story to Walter.

"Mishka Malone, a mysterious newcomer playing in her first game for the Wildcats, scored 15 points on perfect 6-for-6 shooting from the field. All six field goals were spectacular.

"Malone dropped in three long 3-pointers and actually dunked the ball three times. She also had eight steals and nine assists for the Cats, despite playing less than half the game.

"Wildcat Coach Christine Webber hid her star reserve after the win and refused to talk about her. Webber's only comment was, 'It looks like we might have a pretty good season after all.'"

The man with the icy blues looked up from the paper and smiled. It was not a very nice smile. "Well, Walter, what do you make of that? I wonder who that girl might be?" The smile suggested that he had already made a guess.

"Why ask me?" Walter bluffed, but inwardly he shivered. How many girls are named Mishka? It couldn't be a coincidence.

Mr. Ice smiled again and picked at his dry toast and yogurt. They sat at the breakfast table, where they had sat every morning for the past two weeks. Mr. Ice had been polite at all times, but Walter remembered what Dum and Dee told him. Mr. Ice was always nice to those he planned to hurt.

He'd not given anything away. He was sure of that. But he knew Mr. Ice had put the word out and was digging for information. How close was he getting? Would this article give him the clue he needed?

"I just thought you might know her," Mr. Ice said.

Walter forced himself to look into the cold, pale eyes and say, "I've never known anyone named Malone in my life." And that part, at least, was true.

"Perhaps," said Mr. Ice, "but the late Honky and Tonk mentioned a girl about that size. I think a little research might turn up something interesting." He pushed a button under the table and Dum and Dee appeared. Mr. Ice smiled at them, which made Dum and Dee nervous.

"Don't be upset, Boys," Mr. Ice said in the tone of a purring cat. "I just want you to do a little job for me."

"On him?" asked Dee, pointing to Walter. "Be glad to!"

"No," he answered. "We've got more than a week before we have to do that. I told Walter that I was clever enough to find her without forcing him to talk. And now I think I have."

He tossed the sports page to Dum and said, "Read that, Dummy, and tell me what you think."

Dum frowned and then read, "'49ers Stop Packers, 27-13.' Geez, Boss, are we looking for a football player?"

"Not *that* story, you idiot! Read the one I marked!"

Dum read through the article, mumbling to himself as he did. "I don't get it," he said after several minutes.

Walter had no trouble believing that. It had not taken him long to realize that Dum and Dee had been hired for their muscle and not their brains.

"I'll bet that girl is the one we want," said Mr. Ice. "So I want you to find out as much about her as you can."

"You want us to grab her?" asked Dee.

"No. Not yet. We have to be sure she's the right one."

"How we gonna find that out?" Dum asked. "We ain't even got a picture of her."

"Why do I always have to tell you how to do your jobs?" Mr. Ice complained. "She's on a basketball team, isn't she? Teams practice, don't they? She was in the paper, wasn't she? So reporters will be covering the practices, won't they?"

"Aha!" said Dee as the light slowly dawned. "You want us to play reporter, right?"

"Wrong, you moron! You're going to be reporters. Only you're going to report to me!"

"What do you want us to report?" Dum asked.

Mr. Ice ticked off the points on his fingers. "What she looks like, get a picture if you can. Where she lives. Who her friends are. And I want to know everywhere she goes and when. Take turns on the shadowing, so she doesn't get suspicious. I'll want your first report tonight!"

The pale, cold eyes suddenly turned on Walter. "Unless you want to save us time and trouble by admitting she's the one."

"I've never known anyone named Malone in my life," Walter again replied, but he knew Mr. Ice was closing in on the truth.

"I thought you'd say that," Mr. Ice replied as Dum and Dee hurried out. "Once those two thugs are told what to do, they can do it pretty well. We should have some news by tonight. Now, let's get you your breakfast."

He pushed the button again and Mrs. Grey flitted into the room, still looking like a ghost. Walter assumed that she changed her clothes now and then, but in two weeks he had never seen her in any other color. Her feet never made a sound, and she never said anything.

She served him and then left without a word. Walter heard a car start up and looked out the window to see Dum and Dee drive off through the gate.

He was now alone with Mr. Ice. The man was bigger, but not by much. Walter was younger, faster and probably almost as strong. There was no sign that Mr. Ice was carrying a gun. Walter thought, could I jump him and get away before an alarm is raised?

Mr. Ice smiled and reached under the table again. Walter felt a hand on his shoulder. He looked up and saw the dog handler.

"Don't even think about it!" the man said.

"Dodo here will look after you while Dum and Dee are gone," Mr. Ice said. "It was a good thought, Walter, but your eyes gave you away. They always do."

Mr. Ice looked at his dry toast and yogurt for a few moments, then pushed the plate away. "I'm not hungry," he admitted. "It always happens when I have work to do. Enjoy yourself, Walter. I'll see you this evening, and we'll find out what Dum and Dee have learned."

"Whadaya want me to do with him?" Dodo asked.

"Be nice to him, unless he makes trouble. Take him outside for a while. The poor boy hasn't been outside in two weeks. Just be careful. He's thinking all the time. I can tell. People who think a lot can be dangerous."

He gave Walter a cold smile and added, "Dodo is also a lot smarter than the bird he was named for. Be a good boy, Walter. I need you in one piece, for the time being!"

"I'll take my gun along in case he gets cute and tries to make a run for it," Dodo said.

"Numskull!" snarled Mr. Ice. "If you shoot him, you could very well kill him! And I need him alive for the big night coming up! My own boss is counting on it!"

"Then what do I do if he tries to run?"

"Take a couple of the dogs along. That should stop him from trying anything foolish. Just make sure they don't maul him too much if he does. I want his hide in good condition!"

The iceberg eyes shifted to Walter and the smile reappeared. "But you won't try anything foolish, will you, Walter? No, I think you're much too smart for that."

So, for the first time in two weeks, Walter stepped outside the house. It was a beautiful late autumn day. Thanksgiving had just passed, and Mr. Ice and his household had not bothered to celebrate it. Christmas was less than a month away.

The full moon, however, arrived before Christmas. If Walter wanted to live to celebrate the holidays, he would have to think of something fast!

What could he do? Dodo was unarmed. Walter could probably outrun him, but not the two dogs that trotted along with him. Maybe if they got close enough to the fence, he could scramble over before they grabbed him. Then he could make a dash for the road and flag down a car...

"That's far enough, Walter!" Dodo said. "You're not gonna get within a hundred yards of that fence!"

So much for that plan.

Relax and think, Walter told himself. I still have time. I can come up with something.

He thought about the article. The girl had to be his Mishka. The name was too rare for anyone else in town to have it. Someone must have given her a last name and enrolled her in school. Maybe she was in foster care.

Dunking a basketball? Walter knew her height, a quarter inch under five feet. She would have to jump nearly her own height straight up to do that!

Then he remembered when he was a mouse how far and how high he could leap. Could he still do it as a human? There was a tree up ahead. He would try a little experiment.

As they passed under the tree, Walter suddenly leaped as high as he could. His hands closed over a branch, and he swung his heels up over his head before Dodo or the dogs could react. He balanced himself on the limb and looked down at them.

Dodo stared, then laughed. "Nice jump, Walter!" he said, "but where does it get you? Now you can either come down like a good boy or I'll have the dogs hold you here while I go get a chainsaw and cut down the tree. Your choice."

Walter dropped back to the ground and looked up to where he'd leaped. It was a good jump. He must have had three feet of air under his shoes when he grabbed the branch. Mishka would have had even more. It had to be her!

"Relax," he told Dodo. "I've been penned up in that house so long I feel like an animal in a zoo. Don't you think you'd feel the same way?"

"Okay, but you stay outa trees. Mr. Ice don't like having his trees cut down. Makes him real mad. You don't want to make him mad, Walter, believe me!"

The jump gave Walter something he'd lacked before: confidence. He was stronger now, no doubt of that. And he was faster and quicker too! A chance would come. Maybe only for a minute. Maybe only for a few seconds...

But it would come and he would be ready for it!

Walter tried to relax and enjoy being outdoors. The sky was clear; the air was chilly. The grass was still crisp from an early morning frost. He was almost grateful for the warm jacket Mr. Ice had given him.

Almost, but not quite.

Mr. Ice had supplied him with warm clothes, kept him well-fed and provided a supply of books for reading. Walter had never been much of a reader in school, but now he was beginning to like it.

Of course, his choices were limited. There was no television, no radio, no music of any kind throughout the house. The grounds, he decided, were like a well-cared-for cemetery. They were attractive yet depressing. There was no real life or joy on the property.

Sometimes visitors came to see Mr. Ice. Whenever that happened, Walter was sent to his room and locked in. At other times, during the day, he had the run of the house, but Dum or Dee or both were always with him.

Who were these visitors and what was their business? Walter knew it wasn't good. Mr. Ice, he thought, was as close to pure evil as a person could be.

There were people in Walter's life that he disliked, school bullies and a couple of abusive foster parents. But always, there was still something good in them. Sometimes it was very hard to find.

There was nothing good about Mr. Ice. His manners and soft voice were a cruel joke. He was kind only to those he planned to harm, and he was mean and abusive to everyone else. He made his money through ruining people's lives.

Of course, he hired others to do the dirty work while he kept his own hands clean. And, when the work was done and the dirty hands no longer needed, he would...

Walter thought of Honky and Tonk and shivered.

"I'd never dream of shooting a person," Mr. Ice had told him. "But where is it against the law to shoot a couple of mice?"

Walter learned an important lesson. Evil could wear nice clothes, live in a nice house, speak softly and have proper manners. But evil would always be evil, no matter where it lived or how it dressed.

Now, could he live long enough to put that lesson to good use?

Just six months ago he had met the old woman and this whole set of adventures had begun. Now, she was gone from his life. He remembered her words:

"From now on, your life will never be boring."

Unfortunately, she had *not* told Walter how long his life would be...

"Time to go back," Dodo said.

"Who says so?" Walter asked.

"*I* say so!" Dodo replied. He was a few shades brighter than Dum and Dee, but he was never going to win any prizes on quiz shows. He seemed fond of his dogs, but cared nothing about people.

That seemed to be true of everyone who worked for Mr. Ice. The thought depressed Walter and turned the beautiful morning into a teasing mirage as they returned to the house.

Mr. Ice had gone out. Walter was locked in his room. He fell on the bed and picked up a book he'd been reading. A slip of paper fell out. There was writing on it.

"Don't give up hope," Walter read. "Your friends now know where you are. Be brave and ready when the time comes. Destroy this note and say nothing to anyone." The note was unsigned.

Walter tore the note to pieces and flushed them down the toilet. Then he picked up the book and tried to read.

Someone here was on his side. Who?

CHAPTER TEN

Fairness, Fish and Bravery

"We've got some good news and some bad news," Phipps said that night to Mishka, Pomona Mona and Officer Mulholand. "Which do you want first?"

"The good news, of course!" Pomona Mona snapped.

"Okay then," Phipps replied. "Walter is alive and well and we know where he is."

"That's wonderful!" Mishka cried. The heavy feeling that sometimes settled over her like a blanket seemed to lift and float away. This is what happiness feels like, she thought.

"What's the bad news?" Mulholand asked suspiciously.

"We can't get to him," Phipps admitted. "Not yet, at any rate. That's part of it."

"You mean there's more?" Pomona Mona asked.

"There is," Phipps said. "We think the people holding Walter may want to kidnap Mishka too."

Pomona Mona's eyes blazed with a fury they had not shown since her days on the circuit with the Bombers. "They want to grab *my* little girl?" she bellowed. "After I promised poor John on his deathbed that I'd take care of her!"

"How could you do that?' Mulholand wondered. "John Malone never existed. He's just... well..."

"A figure of speech?" Mishka added helpfully.

"Don't matter!" Pomona Mona said. "If he *had* existed, I woulda made that promise. Nobody messes with my little niece unless they get past me first! A lotta skaters tried that in the old days, and they found out you don't mess with Pomona Mona! No sir!"

"But where is Walter?" Mishka asked Phipps.

"He's being held in a house on that property next to the wetland you visited a few weeks ago," Phipps answered. "We've had our eye on the man who lives there for some time. We even planted an agent in his house a few months ago."

"Then why didn't we know sooner?" Mulholand asked.

"The agent couldn't get a message out until today," Phipps said. "Everybody there is suspicious of everybody else. They watch each other all the time."

"Well," Mulholand grumbled, "if Walter's being held there, then let's get a warrant, go out and get him and charge the kidnappers."

"Not that easy," Phipps replied. "Walter's being guarded all the time. The guards have orders to shoot him and hide the body if we make any sudden move. We've got to plan things carefully if we want to get him out alive. Besides..."

"Just a cotton-pickin' minute here!" Pomona Mona interrupted. "Those dirty so-and-sos musta grabbed Walter 'cause he snooped around and saw somethin'. But what do they want with Mishka?"

"She knows where those two hitmice came from," Phipps said. "She saw them as humans and could identify pictures. By the way, our agent says they've been shot."

"Why, that's murder!" Pomona Mona exclaimed.

"I'm afraid it isn't, and that's our problem," Phipps said. "Murder only applies to humans. They were mice. They don't count."

"This is all very strange," Mishka said yet again. Do you mean that if someone hurts me while I'm a girl, then it's a crime? But if someone hurts me while I'm a mouse, then it's not? Even though it's the same me?"

"I'm afraid so," Phipps replied. "It may not make much sense, but it's the law."

"If the law says that, then the law's a jerk," Pomona Mona snorted. "Who are these creeps holdin' poor Walter anyway?"

"The property owner goes by the name of Mr. Ice," Phipps said. "We're pretty sure he's mixed up in some very nasty business, but so far we haven't been able to prove anything. He's always been clever enough to stay just out of our reach."

Mishka was thinking. "Walter told me once about the time he found a stash of illegal drugs and destroyed them. Do you think that's why they were after him?"

"That's probably what's behind it," Phipps said. "This Mr. Ice is a big supplier. We know it, but we can't prove it. Not yet. We can catch the street dealers, but there's never any way we can tie them to him. And as fast as we arrest them, new ones take their place."

This is what humans call a problem, Mishka thought. She was starting to realize that life for humans was full of problems. When she first became a girl, she thought that humans would never worry about anything. After all, they had enough to eat and no predators around to eat them.

But now she realized she was wrong.

"If you know Walter's there, why don't you just charge in and get him before they know what's happening?" Pomona Mona asked.

"We'd have to get a warrant first," Phipps explained. "That means we'd have to tell the judge that it was a gigantic mouse that was kidnapped, or maybe mousenapped, and the mouse was probably trespassing when it was grabbed. The judge would then ask us if we thought that mousenapping was against the law."

"Well, don't it become illegal as soon as Walter becomes human again?" Pomona Mona asked.

"Oh boy! The lawyers are going to have all kinds of fun with that one!" Mulholand guessed.

"By the time it gets argued through the courts, it could take more than a year," Phipps said. "We haven't got a year. We don't even have a month. When do you become a mouse again?" he asked Mishka.

"Just a few more days," Mishka said. She was trying her best to understand human worries and problems, but it was very hard. What were these things called laws? Were they like rules? Did that mean that breaking into a house was like dribbling a basketball? Was it okay as long as you did it a certain way? Did a judge wear a whistle like a referee and blow it when you did something wrong?

Would Mr. Ice get to shoot a free throw if they broke into his house the wrong way?

Life as a human was getting more weird all the time.

"I think we can get this guy and rescue Walter," Phipps said. "But Mishka, we're going to need your help."

"What do you want me to do?" Mishka asked.

"We think Mr. Ice has a couple of spies watching you," Phipps explained. "They're trying to make sure you're the girl Mr. Ice wants, that you are the fourth giant mouse. We want you to show him that you are."

"How?" Mishka asked.

"Drop the low profile," Phipps said. "You'll have reporters covering practice tomorrow. The spies might be among them. Go ahead and dunk the ball. And I'm going to tell your coach to let you score 40 points in your next game."

"What about the poor team they're playin' against?" Pomona Mona asked. "Is it fair to run up the score like that?"

Mishka frowned. Here was another human thing she had to learn. What did "fair" mean? She had heard people say that life wasn't fair sometimes. But she had known from the time she was born that fairness didn't apply to something as low on the food chain as a mouse. It never had, and it never would.

Life was life and death was death, and all mice had to take their chances. The stronger, quicker, luckier mice lived; the others didn't. Fairness had nothing to do with it.

Humans seemed to worry about fairness all the time. They all seemed to need something to complain about. Acey complained about her leg, even though it was getting better every day. She had no predators after her, and her boyfriend Sean carried all her things. "You're safe, you're warm and you're full," Mishka said to her one day at lunch. "Isn't that enough?"

Acey gave her a puzzled look and said nothing.

Mio liked to worry. She worried about her grades, her activities, her performance on the team. But her grades were perfect. She had all the activities she could ever want, and she was a starter on the team. Still she wasn't happy.

"You're faster, quicker and stronger than I am," she told Mishka after practice. "I can't defend you, and I can't get around you, no matter how hard I try."

"We're on the same team, so it doesn't matter," Mishka said.

Mio gave her a puzzled look and said, "It matters to me."

Shawana worried because she was one of very few black students at the school. "We need more sisters here," she grumbled.

But you have Joe, and you called me a sister once," Mishka said. "Don't I count?"

"You kinda count," Shawana admitted. "I like you, Girl, but you're just too light to be the real thing."

"Suppose I change?" Mishka asked.

This time Shawana gave her an inquisitive look and said, "You can't change, Girl! Nobody can. You are what you are and that's that!"

But I am *not* always what I am, Mishka realized. I have two bodies. That makes me different from everybody except Walter. They can sense I'm different, even though they don't know how. That's why I'm strange to them.

All this went through her mind while Phipps spoke. "We have a plan to get Walter back," he was saying, "but we want to do more than that. We want to shut down Mr. Ice and his whole operation."

"How do you plan to do that?" Mulholand asked. "We can nab the little fish. Mr. Ice is a medium fish. But if you want that operation closed down, you'll have to catch the big fish."

Mishka blinked. What was all this talk about fish? It must be another figure of speech. Humans!

"Exactly!" said Phipps. "Our agent sent word that a big fish is coming. He wants Walter's hide as a coat for his lady friend. That's why they're keeping him prisoner. They're waiting for him to turn into a mouse again."

"I wouldn't call 'em fish!" Pomona Mona growled. "They sound more like a bunch of dirty snakes!"

"I agree," said Phipps. "Unfortunately, Mishka, they want your hide too!"

Mishka felt a spark of fear. Humans did have predators, just like other animals. Humans *were* predators, and they preyed on one another.

"Can't the law stop 'em?" Pomona Mona asked.

"If they grab her now, yes. If they wait until she's a mouse, no. There's nothing in the law to protect mice."

"What about the endangered species act?" Mulholand asked.

"We've applied to have the weremouse and the mousewere added to the list," Phipps said. "The studies and the paperwork will be completed sometime late next year."

"That sure doesn't do us much good now!" Mulholand commented.

"Right," Phipps agreed. "So we let them grab Mishka while she is still a girl. *That's* clearly against the law. If they grab her, then we can grab them."

"You want to *let* them grab my little niece?" Pomona Mona cried. "After I promised poor John I'd look after her!"

"Aunt Mona, John Malone never existed," Mishka reminded her.

"Don't matter! My job is to keep you safe," Pomona Mona said.

"But you can't keep her safe unless we get the people who are after her," Mulholand said. "If we scare them off, they'll just come back and try again. We've got to catch them; and to catch fish, you need bait."

"And I'm the bait?" Mishka asked.

"Yes," said Phipps. "We can't force you, but if you want a free life, if you want to see Walter again, then you need to trust us."

This was another new thing for Mishka to learn: trust. She knew what the word meant, but she'd had no experience with it. Mice trusted their instinct, and nothing else. Did humans actually trust one another?

"What do you want me to do?" Mishka said.

"Do you have one or two good friends you can trust?" Phipps asked her.

Mishka thought of Acey, Mio and Shawana. "I think so," she said. But could she really trust them? Acey, Mio and Shawana all thought they were different from each other because their skins were of different colors. But it was one skin and one body for each. Mishka had two different skins and two different bodies. Could they understand that? And how would they treat her once they knew?

"Well, stick close to them for the next few days," Phipps told her. "Don't go anywhere by yourself, until I tell you to."

"This is all so peculiar," Mishka said again. "You want me to put myself in danger deliberately?"

"Yes," said Phipps. "Are you brave enough to do it?"

Mishka hesitated. Bravery was another thing she knew nothing about. Mice weren't brave. They weren't built for it. She was human now, and learning human things. Could she learn to be brave too?

Mishka slowly nodded her head. "I'll try," she said.

Notes from a Diary

I never thought that learning to be human would be so hard. Now I have to try to be brave. People tell me that this is hard even for humans. They are not born brave. They have to learn it too.

Humans have to learn all these things called behaviors, and bravery is one of them. I suppose I'll have to learn all the others too. I know it's going to be hard.

Mice don't learn much. Everything we need to know is there when we are born. It's what humans call instinct. The most powerful instinct in a mouse is fear. Even humans have that one.

Aunt Mona says that being brave doesn't mean having no fear. She says it means overcoming the fear you have. She says I'll have to learn to stand when my instinct says to run.

Can humans really do this? Mice can't.

Aunt Mona says some humans can overcome their fear and some can't. I asked her if some humans had no fear at all, and she said that a few might. Then I asked her if this was good, and she said no. She said people like that were more stupid than brave.

"Foolhardy" was the word she used.

It's strange that humans have so many words for the same thing.

I have studied about bravery because I am going to have to learn to be brave. There are all kinds of words for it. I've looked up courage, valor, fearlessness, intrepid, dauntless, grit, mettle and a bunch more. Do they all mean the same thing or are there different kinds of bravery?

I showed this page to Aunt Mona because I didn't know how to finish it. I asked her why people are brave.

She said there were lots of reasons, but the best and most powerful was love. She told me that if you love someone, it's easier to be brave and face danger. Then she told me that she would face danger for me because she loves me!

No one has ever said they loved me before. It makes me feel odd just to think about it. It makes me feel stronger too. I think I could face danger now, if it would help Walter. Yes, I will face danger for him.

Does that mean I love him?

CHAPTER ELEVEN

Words that Hurt

The first night of the full moon was the night of Mishka's next game. All that day she felt nervous and jumpy, not about the game, but about what would happen afterward.

Calamity Chris was puzzled. An FBI agent had visited her and said it would be in the interest of National Security to leave Mishka in the game as long as possible and let her score as many points as she could.

So she did, and Mishka ran wild for the entire first half.

"Girl, that was almost *too* easy!" Shawana said as they returned to the locker room for half-time. "We're up 52-17 with two quarters left to go! How many points has she got, Acey?"

"Thirty," said Acey, who had been helping the scorekeeper, "along with ten rebounds, ten steals and four assists."

"A triple-double in one half?" Shawana asked unbelievingly.

"Perfect from the line and perfect from the field," Acey replied, shaking her head in wonder. "I've never seen a half like that anywhere!"

Shawana agreed. "Girl," she said to Mishka, "you're so bad I wonder if you're even human sometimes!"

Mishka winced at the comment. She had not yet found the courage to tell her friends about her double life. She knew she would have to do it very soon now. She couldn't ask them to help her if they didn't know the truth.

She tried to think of what to say as they waited for Acey, who was now off crutches, but still hobbling with a brace on her knee. How do I tell Shawana that she's right, Mishka thought. Sometimes I'm *not* a human being!

Calamity Chris was smiling for once. "No way they can make up 35 points in one half," she said. "We'll start the reserves and let them play the rest of the way. I'll put Shawana or Mio back in if they make a run at us, but Mishka, you're done for the night."

"There're TV crews all over the gym," Acey reported. "You're going to be on the eleven o'clock news tonight, Mishka!"

"And no ducking the reporters this time either!" Shawana added.

"I know," Mishka said. "Did you see the two that have been hanging around the gym all week? Are they here?"

"Those two?" Shawana asked. "Girl, those are two you don't want to talk to! They give me the absolute creeps!"

"I heard them call each other Dum and Dee," Mio added. "They sure don't look much like reporters to me!"

"They don't act like reporters either," said Acey. "They follow us back to your place every night. It's like they were trying to get you alone."

"And not for no interview neither!" Shawana put in. "Girl, I got the feeling those two are ba-ad news!"

"That's why I've got to meet them," Mishka said.

"What?" Shawana nearly shouted. "You want to meet those two?"

"Yes!" Mishka said. "But they can't know it's what I want. That's where I need your help!"

"Ahem!" said the coach. "Would you four please let me know when you're ready to go back out and play ball? The game isn't *quite* over yet!"

Mishka decided that this would have to be the time. After the game, she'd be swarmed over by reporters, and she had to tell her friends what was going to happen.

"Can I talk to Shawana, Mio and Acey alone for a minute?" she asked. "I won't take long. It's really important!"

The coach frowned, then nodded. "Make it fast," she said. "I don't like starting short-handed."

The rest of the team filed out, and Mishka was alone with her three friends. She took a deep breath and wondered how to begin.

"Shawana," she finally said. "Remember what you said on the way in? About wondering if I'm human? Well, in a way, you're right! I'm not, sometimes!"

"Girl, what *are* you talking about?" Shawana asked.

"Remember that stuff on the news about the two giant mice?"

"Yeah," said Acey. "They disappeared. No one knows where."

"Well, there weren't two," Mishka said. "There were four, and I'm the fourth. The other three were weremice, and I'm a mousewere. So I'm not really human after all."

"You sure look human!" Acey protested.

"Wait a sec," said Mio. "Two giant mice were caught and then disappeared. You say you're the fourth. Who's the third?"

"My boyfriend," Mishka answered. "His name is Walter. He saved my life once."

"You got a boyfriend?" Shawana asked. "How come you never told us anything about him?"

"Because he's disappeared too," Mishka said.

"Look," said Mio. "Do us all a favor. Start at the beginning and tell us everything. We've got time."

So Mishka told them all she knew, about being saved from the cat, learning in the Bagshott Room, growing up in a couple of weeks, the fight with the hitmice and returning to her mouse form every month during the full moon. Finally, she told them about her new identity and Walter's disappearance near the mysterious fence.

"Whoa!" Shawana said when she finished. "This is the strangest half-time of my life!"

"Is this really true?" Acey asked.

"I believe her," Mio said, "but where do we come in?

"I need your help tonight," Mishka said.

"How?" they all asked at once.

"Those two so-called reporters work for the man who has Walter," Mishka said. "They want to grab me too. I'm to give them their chance, but it has to be before midnight. Will you help?"

"*Help* some creeps grab you?" Acey asked. "Why?"

"If they get me when I'm a mouse, that's not against the law. Mice have no rights, but girls do. If they grab me while I'm human, then the police and the FBI can go after them."

"What do you want us to do?" Shawana asked.

"Get in a fight with me after the game," Mishka said. "Yell at me. Call me names. Hit me, if you want! Then go off and leave me alone. Just make sure they see it happen. Then they won't be suspicious when I'm suddenly all by myself."

A player stuck her head in the doorway. "Coach needs you all out there now," she said.

"Will you do it?" Mishka asked her friends.

"Girl, I never claimed to be no actress," Shawana said. "But if you want me to get mad, I'll do it!"

"Okay," said Mio. "Let's get out there and finish the game."

"Mio, I'll need your help with something too," Mishka added.

The other team did cut into the lead, but not enough to make a difference. The Wildcats won by 20 and whooped and yelled all the way back to the locker room.

"There're reporters all over the place, and I can't hide you this time," said Calamity Chris. "I told 'em I'd send you out as soon as you got cleaned up. Shawana, Mio and Acey can go with you."

The girls tried to work out a plan as they showered and dressed. "The real reporters will leave right after the interview," Mio said as she helped Mishka fix her hair. "They've got deadlines to meet. So we'll save the show for afterward, when only the two creepies are around to see it."

"Sounds good," Shawana agreed. "Let's go meet the media."

The click and whir of cameras and the brightness of the TV lights took them all by surprise. Reporters shoved microphones in Mishka's face and fired questions at her. A wave of mouselike fear swept over her and she shrank back, but Shawana took her by the shoulders and steadied her.

"Easy, Girl!" she whispered. "Just answer 'em one at a time."

"How did you learn to jump so high?" one reporter asked.

"Lots of practice," Mishka answered, "and, uh, my mom and dad helped me a lot."

"Were they up in the stands tonight?"

Mishka tried to look sad. "No, they're both dead," she replied. "I'm an orphan. But I'm sure they were watching from somewhere."

She almost smiled as she said it. What would her real mother and father think of their daughter right now, assuming mice could think? And were they really somewhere? What was this thing called heaven that people talked about?

Before she could think about it, another reporter fired a question at her. "Do you play other sports too?"

Mishka shrugged. "I don't know. I might."

"Where do you come from?"

That one was easy. "A very small place in West Virginia," she said. "My grandmother brought me up after my parents were killed in a train wreck in Bulgaria. Now she's dead too."

"What's your favorite subject?" another reporter asked.

Mishka had been hoping for that one. She looked around and spotted the two suspects standing at the back of the group.

"Biology," she answered, looking straight at them. "I love mice, and I plan to become the world's greatest expert on them, especially that new giant kind they had here a little while ago."

More questions followed. Mishka answered them, but kept her eyes on the two suspects. They never asked questions and they never took notes. Yet they were watching her, watching the way a pair of snakes might watch a mouse they planned to eat.

They know, she realized. They're ready to make their move...

Shawana, Mio and Acey were asked one question each, and then the interview was over. The reporters packed their equipment and left. All but two, that is.

"Ready for the show?" Shawana asked.

"Yes," Mishka replied. "Let's go outside. They'll follow us. We'll stage it in the parking lot."

The last cars were driving off as the four teammates left the gym by the side door. The lot was empty and dark, with just a couple of faint lights at the far end. The full moon shone briefly between breaks in the clouds.

Mishka checked her watch. She would transform in just over an hour. There was no time to lose!

She gave Shawana a sudden shove and cried out, "What do you mean by that?"

Shawana took up her cue. "I mean what I say, Mouse!" she yelled back. "Don't you go saying things about me!"

"Yeah?" Mishka replied. "And what did you just call me?"

"Dumb little hick from West Virginia! That's what you'd like people to think, isn't it?" Shawana shouted. Mishka trembled a bit. Shawana was a pretty good actress after all. "Well, I know better. I know where you really come from!"

Shawana stamped her foot in mock rage and then whispered to Mio, "How'm I doing? Can they hear us?"

"Perfect!" Mio whispered back. She was standing between them and pretending to act as a peacemaker. "Okay, Mishka. You know what to say next."

"I can't call her that!" Mishka whispered back as she pretended to struggle. "It's awful!"

"Go ahead and say it, Girl!" Shawana muttered. "This has got to sound good or they won't go for it!"

Mishka shuddered. "Okay," she whispered, and then her voice rose to a shout.

"You're calling *me* dumb?" She nearly choked, but forced the next words out. "You, you stupid nigger!"

Then her voice dropped back to a whisper. "I'm sorry, Shawana! You know I don't mean it!"

"That's okay, Girl," Shawana whispered back to her. "I don't really mean this either!" Then she threw a punch at Mishka's head.

Mishka didn't move. Her reflexes were quick enough to get her out of the way, but she stood still and let Shawana connect. Shawana opened her hand at the last instant, so the blow was more of a slap than a punch. But it still packed enough power to stagger her.

Acey grabbed Shawana's arms, while Mio pushed Mishka away. "We got their attention all right," she muttered. "They're in the shadow of that building over there."

"C'mon, Mio!" Shawana shouted. "I don't like hanging around mousy trash! She ain't a real human being! You coming, Acey?"

Acey looked at Mishka, winked and then turned her back. "I'm with you guys!" she announced loudly. "Little Miss All-Star can walk home alone. I hope the big, bad wolf gets her!"

Mishka walked slowly out to the street, knowing that the two men would follow. The slap had hurt, but the words seemed to hurt even more. Mice had no language. They never fought with words.

The pain and hurt in Shawana's eyes had been real, even though she knew Mishka had not meant what she said. Words hurt. Language can be cruel, and humans are a very strange breed.

"Hey, Mishka!" A voice called to her from the street.

Mishka turned. It was the two so-called reporters. They were sitting in a car. The engine was running.

"Could you answer a couple more questions?" one of them asked.

Mishka forced herself to smile. "Of course," she said. "You were at the game, weren't you?"

"Yeah. We covered it for our, uh, paper. You were great! Did you just have a fight with your friends?"

"They're not my friends anymore!" Mishka replied.

"They shouldn't have walked off and left you alone like that," the other man said. "It can be dangerous out here. Why don't you get in and we'll give you a ride home?"

Of course, Mishka had been warned about accepting rides from strangers, and her mouse instinct made her shy away from them anyway. She knew that a girl getting into a car with a stranger was like a mouse choosing to play with a cat. The game ends with a full cat and a well-digested mouse. Some people are predators, and their prey are other people.

But now she had to go against the warnings and her own instincts. She would act like a dumb little girl from another state, although she was sure that *real* West Virginia girls, even dumb ones, would know better than to try what she was going to do.

Mishka forced another smile. "Sure," she said, and got into the car.

CHAPTER TWELVE

Meanwhile... Meanwhile...

Even as the car door slammed shut behind Mishka, Mio was on the phone. She punched in the number Mishka had given her and said, "They went for it. She's wearing the bug and she's in the car. Hurry!"

"Understood," said the special dispatcher. "Mulholand cleared for immediate EMD. All units stand by to implement EMRP."

The Emergency Mouse Rescue Plan was under way.

Another car raced into the parking lot and squealed to a stop beside Shawana and Acey. Phipps jumped out and displayed his FBI badge. "Did it work?" he asked.

"It worked, but I don't like it!" Shawana said. "She's in a car with two of the worst creeps I've ever seen!"

"Believe me, they're angels compared to their boss," Phipps replied. "You girls did well. Better get back in the gym and call your folks to come get you."

Instead, Shawana opened the back door and jumped in the car. "No way!" she said. "I helped Mishka get into this mess, and I'm gonna help her get out!"

"That goes for me too," said Mio as she came running back.

"Can you use a girl with a gimpy leg?" Acey asked.

"This is against every regulation I can think of, but we might be able to use you anyway," Phipps said as Mio and Acey piled in after Shawana. "Fasten your seat belts!" Phipps was tearing out of the lot before they got the door shut.

"EMD Two to EMD One," he called into the radio. "On my way with an extra load."

"EMD One to EMD Two," the voice of Officer Mulholand replied. "I copy. Have an extra load myself. Are you there, EMD Three?"

"EMD Three, check." It was Patrolman Rizzo, the handler of Finigan, the tracking dog. "Finigan's gonna want over-time for this. His contract doesn't call for night work."

"We'll get him a date with a French poodle if he helps us bring this off," Mulholand responded. "What is your extra load, EMD Two?"

"Three basketball players," said Phipps. "What about you?"

"Pomona Mona and Ivon. They jumped in the cruiser and wouldn't get out. What about you, EMD Three?"

"Just Finigan, and that's enough," said Rizzo. "He slobbers."

And so the three cars of the Emergency Mouse Rescue Team sped out of town carrying the world's most unusual posse: two policemen, one FBI agent, a former roller-derby star, a Bulgarian baker, three basketball players and a dog that did not like to work overtime.

"Hurry, Herbert!" Pomona Mona urged. "Cousin John would never forgive me if I let anything happen to his little girl!"

Mulholand did not bother to remind her that John Malone had never existed.

Meanwhile, Mishka was trying to act like a silly little girl who was just beginning to realize that she was in big trouble. "Hey!" she said to Dum and Dee. "This isn't the way back to my place! Where are we going?"

"Relax, Honey," said Dum. "We said we'd take you home, and we will. We just didn't say which home!"

"You're gonna come out to our place and have a little visit with our boss," Dee added. "Okay?"

"It is *not* okay!" Mishka said. "Stop the car and let me out right now!"

"Not a chance!" said Dum. He took a small pistol from a pocket in his coat and tapped Mishka on the arm with it. "Now, you just sit real still and you might get there in one piece. Mr. Ice does want you in one piece, for the time being!"

Mishka looked from one to the other. She realized they were toying with her, just like Rancid the Cat had toyed with her when she was a tiny mouse trapped on Pomona Mona's cellar steps. Walter had rescued her then. Now she was helping rescue him. Someone else was going to have to rescue them both.

Life as a human was getting more strange and frightening.

At Mr. Ice's, Walter sat at a kitchen table with a piece of pie on a plate in front of him. He had only managed two bites. "Eat up!" Mr. Ice urged with an icy smile. "You know I can't have stuff like that anymore; it makes me feel good to see others enjoy it."

Walter knew by now that the only thing Mr. Ice really enjoyed was watching others suffer. He wants to see my fear. Well, I'm not going to let him! Walter forced himself to smile back and eat the pie, slowly, every crumb of it.

"That was pretty good," he said after the last bite had disappeared. "Mrs. Grey is getting better." In fact, he had not tasted it at all and didn't even know what kind it had been.

"You're a brave boy," Mr. Ice admitted. "It's too bad I couldn't have you work for me." He smiled again, and his eyes glinted like two pale icebergs on a calm, flat sea. "My boss is coming tonight in person. If you find me frightening, Walter, just wait till you meet him!"

In the night beyond the house, five cars sped toward Mr. Ice's large, cold house.

In the first car, Mishka sat between Dum and Dee and no longer had to act frightened. She knew these two creeps were just humans, but she could imagine them changing into giant cats when she became a mouse again. She was in trouble now, and there was no backing out. Would the others come through for her?

In the second car, Shawana, Mio and Acey were wondering if they had made the right choice. They had left the city and were out in open country. Clouds covered the full moon. The roads grew narrower and bumpier. The headlights reflected the gleams of eyes as night creatures scurried out of the way.

Phipps drove on without saying a word.

In the third car, Pomona Mona kept urging Mulholand to go faster. "My niece is in the hands of kidnappers and murderers!" she cried. "If they harm so much as one hair on her little head..." She clenched her teeth and clutched the only weapon she'd had time to grab, an old softball bat.

"Don't worry," Ivon tried to calm her. "We have time. The *prestupniks* dare not harm them before midnight."

"But what if one of them makes a mistake? What if their clock is fast? What if..."

"Calm yourself, Mona Honey," Mulholand reassured her. "Officer Herbert J. Mulholand is on the case!"

Pomona Mona nearly told him that was the reason she *was* worried. But she realized that he had called her "Honey!" He really cared about her! It wasn't just the chili dogs, after all.

In the fourth car, a sad-eyed Rizzo tried to cheer up a sad-eyed bloodhound. "It's our big chance, Finigan!" he kept re-peating. "If we bring this off, we could make the cover of *People* and maybe even be on *Oprah*! Think of it! You could be Dog of the Year!"

Finigan gave a bored yawn. He would work overtime, if Rizzo insisted, but the price was four Doggie-Crisps per hour, half in advance. The thought made him lick his chops and slobber on the seat cushions.

In a fifth car, a man sat staring straight ahead while his chauffeur drove. He was bigger than Mr. Ice, and his eyes were even colder.

He also wore a fancy coat made from very unusual fur.

The hands on the clock crept closer to midnight.

Dum and Dee, along with Mishka, were the first to reach the big, cold house where Mr. Ice was waiting. The car screeched to a stop, and the two of them pulled Mishka out and marched her inside.

"Well! What have we here?" asked Mr. Ice. "You two actually managed to do something right! Did she give you any trouble?"

"Nah!" said Dee. "She had a fight with her friends and they left her all alone. Easy as picking up a stray dime."

"Told her we was reporters and she jumped right in," Dum added.

"Oldest trick in the book and you fell for it, didn't ya, Kid?" He gave Mishka a dig in the ribs with his gun.

"Careful with that thing, you nincompoop!" roared Mr. Ice. Dum and Dee looked relieved. They did not like to have Mr. Ice smiling at them.

Mr. Ice then smiled at Mishka. "So you are the famous new basketball star, Mishka Malone, eh?" he said in a voice that was almost pleasant. "It's a pleasure to have you as my guest."

"What are you going to do with me?" Mishka demanded.

"I'm going to reunite you with an old friend," Mr. Ice replied. "I believe you know a boy named Walter, don't you?"

"W... Walter? I..."

"Never mind," said Mr. Ice with another cold smile. "Your eyes just told me everything I need to know. Walter's an old friend, isn't he? Or maybe a new friend, but you *do* know him."

Why, he seems almost nice, Mishka thought. Maybe he's not going to harm us after all. She did not know what Walter had learned about Mr. Ice's smiles.

As if guessing her thoughts, Mr. Ice raised a hand. "I promise you that no harm will come to Mishka Malone or Walter Wampler," he said. "I'm simply going to enjoy your company for a while tonight and see if anything, uh, happens."

He snapped his fingers at Dum and Dee. "Take her in with her friend and keep an eye on them," he ordered. "We have very important company due any minute now!"

Meanwhile, Phipps, Mulholand, Rizzo and the unauthorized posse had pulled up at the edge of the wetland. "Is she up there yet?" Mulholand asked.

"I'm getting a faint signal," Phipps answered. "Where did you hide the transmitter, Mio?"

"In her hair, right by the rubber band on her ponytail. I hope you didn't damage it when you smacked her, Shawana."

"Huh? That was just a little tap," Shawana replied. "If I'd really smacked her one, she'd still be on the ground!"

"Where's the rest of the cops?" Pomona Mona demanded. "Don't tell me we're the whole rescue party!"

"They're keeping back out of sight," Phipps said. "There's a really big fish coming in tonight. They'll seal off the roads behind him and then close in. Mulholand and I'll go up there first, with Rizzo and the dog for backup."

"Why do we have to wait for Mr. Bigfish?" Pomona Mona grumbled. "Why not bust in right now? My little niece..."

"Yes, I know!" said Phipps. "But Bigfish, as you call him, hasn't done anything yet. If we stop his car before he gets there, he can just claim he was out for a moonlight ride. We have nothing to tie him to Mr. Ice."

"But if we can catch him with Walter and Mishka and Mr. Ice," Mulholand put in, "then we've got him, and a whole drug empire will come crashing down!"

"What can we do to help?" Acey asked.

"Stay down here by the wetland," Phipps said. "It's the one weak spot in our circle. Mulholand, Rizzo and I are going in now. Did you bring what I asked?"

Acey handed over Mishka's game jersey. "It's unwashed," she said. "I can smell it myself. But what's the dog for?"

"Backup," Rizzo explained. "The house is full of hiding places, and they may find the transmitter. But they can't hide her from Finigan. Ready to go, boy?"

Finigan slobbered and accepted another Doggie-Crisp.

"Twenty minutes to midnight," Mulholand said. "We'll get as close as we can, then move in as soon as Bigfish arrives. Let's go!"

"Good hunting, Herbert!" Pomona Mona said, and punched him gently on the arm for luck. "You be careful now!"

"I'll be back for more chili dogs, Mona Honey!" Mulholand replied as he moved out into the darkness with Phipps and Rizzo. Ivon grinned and Shawana, Mio and Acey stifled giggles.

Walter and Mishka were together again.

"I'll leave you two alone for a few minutes," Mr. Ice said with a smile that was almost pleasant. "I know you have lots to talk about. But we'll be right outside the door, and there is no other way out. So don't try anything foolish."

"How did you get here?" Walter asked as soon as they were alone.

"I let them catch me," Mishka said. "Don't worry! There's..."

"Shh!" Walter put a hand over her mouth. "The place is probably bugged. Nobody trusts anybody around here."

"But what good would bugs do them? I ate them sometimes when I was a mouse."

"Not that kind of bug," Walter explained. "Microphones. They may even have a video monitor."

"Ah! It's another figure of speech, right? Then how do we talk?" Mishka asked.

"Like this." Walter cupped his hand over Mishka's ear and whispered, "Who is out there?"

Mishka cupped her hand and whispered back, "Mulholand, Rizzo and a man from the FBI. Others too. They have the place surrounded, I think."

"Someone in here is on our side too," Walter whispered. "It might be Dum or Dee or Dodo. Have you met them?"

"Dum and Dee. They grabbed me. What should we do now?"

Before Walter could reply, the door opened and Mr. Ice stepped in. "Sorry to interrupt your little whisper session," he said with a really nasty smile, "but it's almost midnight and our special guest has arrived. He wants to meet you right away!"

The man waiting for them was a bigger, colder version of Mr. Ice. Mishka thought of the figure of speech: a big fish. The man did have the cold look of a fish, like a shark or barracuda.

"These are the two we want?" he said as Mr. Ice brought them in. "Yes," said Mr. Ice, glancing at his watch. "In exactly seven minutes they will become the two biggest mice you've ever seen. Then we can have our little hunt..."

"Hunt?" said Bigfish. "Who said anything about a hunt?"

"Well, I thought..."

"Don't think, you moron! I didn't say nothing about no hunt! I said I wanted 'em for a coat, and that's what I'll have!"

In spite of the terrible danger he was in, Walter nearly smiled at the sight of Mr. Ice cringing before someone else. But one look at Bigfish's face killed his smile instantly.

"I never lost a shipment until these two interfered," Bigfish said. "All I've got out of it so far is one fur coat. Now I'm getting a second one for my lady friend, and there's not gonna be any fooling around with stupid sporting chances either!"

He took a gun from a holster under his coat and leveled it at Mishka. "You!" he ordered. "Take off your clothes!"

CHAPTER THIRTEEN

The Midnight Rescue

M ishka looked straight into the barrel of the gun, folded her arms and said, "No, that is not something I will do."

"Bad choice!" Mr. Ice warned. "He gets very angry when anyone says no to him."

Mishka forced herself to stay calm. It took lots of effort. She wanted to run, panic, beg. Instead, she stood perfectly still. "If he shoots now, then he doesn't get his coat," she said.

"She's right, you know," Mr. Ice said to Bigfish. "It's only a few minutes to midnight. We can deal with the clothes after we deal with them."

"Shut up, you moron!" snarled Bigfish. "I want my enemies naked and groveling and begging for mercy, not that they'll get any!"

"Well, I'm not going to beg," Mishka replied. "I'm still a person, and I decide where and when my clothes come off, and they're *not* coming off here or now!"

Walter folded his arms and said, "That goes for me too!"

Then Bigfish smiled. It was not a pretty sight. "I don't need your foot for the coat," he said, and lowered his aim at Mishka's feet. "Now what's it gonna be? Your duds or the foot?"

Mishka shook her head. "No way!" she said.

Bigfish scowled. His finger tightened on the trigger. Mishka tried to make herself jump, but she seemed paralyzed and unable to move. Then Walter cried, "No!" He flung himself at her feet and wrapped his own body around her legs.

"You'll have to shoot me first!" he cried. "And if you do, no coat for you!"

Mishka wondered, is this what humans call love? She remembered what Pomona Mona had said about people putting their own lives on the line for those they really loved. Walter must love me, she realized.

Bigfish kept the scowl, but shifted his aim. "Doesn't matter to me whose foot I shoot, yours or his," he snarled. "Now what's it gonna be?"

Before she even had time to think, Mishka dropped to the floor and covered Walter's feet. I guess this means I love him too, she decided. They lay wrapped together like two parts of a poorly-made pretzel.

"A very interesting knot," Mr. Ice commented. He kept his voice soft and even, but he was enjoying Bigfish's frustration. "We might have a real problem untying you after midnight."

He glanced at his boss, whose face had turned the color of strawberry jam. "Shall we just leave them like that until midnight?" he asked. "It's only a few more minutes."

"No!" Bigfish growled. "I'm not gonna wait! I'm gonna shoot 'em and skin 'em and turn 'em into fashion statements as humans!" He was now completely out of control and waved the gun at Mr. Ice. "And don't you make no smart remarks about sporting chances," he threatened. "You can be replaced too!"

He leveled the gun at Mishka's head. "You go first!" he said.

Mishka thought quickly. Phipps and Mulholand and the others must be closing in. If she could only buy some time! An extra minute, even a few seconds, might make the difference.

"Wait!" she cried. "Let me get up and I'll do what you want."

"Make it fast and no tricks," Bigfish warned. "I've only got a few minutes to enjoy this!"

Mishka got to her feet and took off her shoes and socks. She didn't mind that and was glad to get rid of them. A mousewere in shoes couldn't move very well.

She put a hand to the top button of her blouse and said, "Do you mind if I turn around? I don't like to see you looking at me that way."

"Not a chance, Kid!" Bigfish snarled. "Now get with it!"

"You're the one without a chance, Slimefish!" said a voice from the doorway. Mishka looked up and saw Phipps and Officer Mulholand moving in with guns drawn.

"How did you get in here?" asked an amazed Mr. Ice. "Where are my guards? Why didn't they warn us?"

That question was answered when Dum, Dee and Dodo were marched into the room in handcuffs. Behind them marched two policemen and Mrs. Grey. "Here's your guard!" she said. "I'm Agent Grey of the DEA. You're all under arrest!"

"That's the Drug Enforcement Administration," Walter whispered to Mishka. "It looks like the good guys got here at last!"

"I'm Phipps of the FBI!" said Phipps. "You're all under arrest by me too!"

"I'm Mulholand of the City Police!" said Officer Mulholand, who did not like to be left out of things. "And I'm putting you all under arrest too!"

"That's an awful lot of arresting!" Mishka commented.

Mr. Ice sighed and raised his hands. "I'll go quietly," he said. "I thought this might happen someday, so I've saved some information that you may find valuable. It could land some even bigger fish. Perhaps we can make a deal."

Bigfish was not ready to go as quietly. He had lowered his gun, but still held it. With one sudden move, he gave Walter a kick that sent him sprawling into Officer Mulholand. At the same time, he grabbed Mishka around the neck, pulled her against him and put the gun to her head.

"Get back and let me through!" he demanded. "One false move and the girl here gets it!"

"Give it up!" Phipps urged. "In three more minutes, she won't be a girl!"

"Girl or mouse, it's all the same to me!" Bigfish replied.

"How far do you think you'll get?" Mulholand asked as he tried to untangle himself from Walter. "We've got the place surrounded."

Bigfish smiled an evil smile. "Then you'll just have to let us through. This girl, or mouse, and I are going for a ride!"

"You're bluffing!" Phipps challenged.

"Think so, huh?" Bigfish suddenly jerked the gun away from Mishka's head and fired one shot. Mr. Ice groaned and sank to the floor.

"*That's* what I do to rats who squeal on me!" he said. "Now get back and let us out or the mousegirl gets it too!"

Mulholand stood his ground, but Phipps shook his head. "We can't take a chance in here," he said. "She's a protected witness and an endangered species as well."

Mulholand frowned and backed away. Bigfish, still holding Mishka, edged toward the door. Meanwhile, Walter ducked behind a sofa and was pulling his clothes off and Mrs. Grey was checking on Mr. Ice.

"He's hurt pretty bad, but he'll live if we get him to a doctor quickly," she said.

"Thought I was a better shot than that," said Bigfish as he backed through the door, still keeping his hold on Mishka. "Well, I won't miss her! Remember that!" And he slammed the door behind him and dragged her to the front entrance.

"Back off!" he warned the troopers and FBI men who had surrounded his car and had his driver in custody. "I'm outa here and nobody tries to follow! Give me a five-minute start and I'll turn her loose. Otherwise..."

"You're not getting in that car!" a trooper warned. "Better give it up now, before something really bad happens!"

Bigfish snarled and looked around desperately. He spotted the golf cart Mr. Ice rode around his estate. The keys were in it. Still holding Mishka, he backed over to the cart, shoved her in, then jumped in himself. The troopers and FBI agents held their fire.

Mishka lay on the floor of the cart, with Bigfish's foot pinning her down. Can he drive this thing and still keep me pinned this way, she wondered. As if in answer, the electric motor started with a soft whir and the cart jerked forward.

The troopers parted to let them through. They knew that Bigfish had his gun trained on Mishka's head. Even if they shot him, he would be able to pull the trigger once. The cart zipped through the gate and onto the road that led past the fence to the wetland.

"How far do you think you're going to get?" Mishka asked. "This thing doesn't go very fast. They'll catch us in their cars in a minute or two."

"Shut up!" growled Bigfish. "You don't think I was dumb enough to come up here without a backup plan, do you?"

"What do you mean?" Mishka asked.

"I mean I got a helicopter with a pilot waiting for me just a couple of miles down this road!" Bigfish said. "By the time they figure things out, we'll be a mile up in the air. Then I'll let you go like I promised, straight down!"

Maybe not, Mishka thought. It's a minute to midnight.

"What the...?" Bigfish cried as two figures suddenly loomed up in front of him. It was Rizzo with Finigan.

"Police!" Rizzo shouted. "Hold it right there."

"Woof!" added Finigan.

Bigfish wasn't about to stop. He fired one wild shot in Rizzo's direction, then steered the cart straight for him. Rizzo dived for the ditch and rolled in the mud, letting go of Finigan's leash as he did. The dog was loose, and at that very instant, midnight struck and Mishka transformed.

The air was suddenly full of mousewere scent. Finigan had smelled something like it when he'd tracked Walter a few months earlier. He threw back his head and let out a howl that echoed clear across the wetland.

"*Boje moi!*" Ivon exclaimed. "What was that?"

"I think I wanna go home!" Acey wailed as she shivered.

"That's Rizzo's dog," Pomona Mona said. "Herbert's in trouble, and my little niece is in the hands of kidnappers and murderers! Stay with the girls, Ivon! I'm goin' after her!"

"Miss Mona! It's dangerous! You shouldn't..."

But Pomona Mona had already grabbed her rollerblades and the softball bat and was sprinting for the road. "John would never forgive me if I let something happen to his little girl!" she cried over her shoulder.

"Miss Mona! John Malone never existed!" Ivon shouted after her. But Pomona Mona had already vanished into the night.

Back at the house, Walter had also transformed. He shot out from behind the couch, hit the door hard enough to burst it open, and tore out of the house and past the astounded troopers and FBI men as fast as he could, following the mousewere

scent that now came to him on the night air. Good! They were traveling upwind!

Mulholand sprinted from the house a few seconds later. "Follow that mouse!" he yelled as he leaped into a squad car. Why weren't they already in pursuit, he wondered. Probably waiting for orders. There was no established procedure for handling mousenappings.

Pomona Mona reached the road just in time to see the lights of the golf cart approaching. She quickly kicked off her shoes and slipped on her rollerblades. Years of skating the circuit with the Bombers had taught her how to change them quickly. She was ready a split second after the cart shot past.

Finigan was running a short distance behind the cart. Pomona Mona grabbed his leash as he passed, raised the bat and yelled, "C'mon, Dog! Run like you've never run before!"

Bigfish looked back and saw them closing in. He fired two quick shots over his shoulder with the hope of scaring them off, but Pomona Mona kept on coming!

Mishka heard the shots and knew that someone was coming to her rescue. She squirmed and tried to get her head free, but Bigfish's foot kept her pinned, and she couldn't reach him with her paws. She had split the seams on her jeans and popped the buttons off her blouse when she transformed, and her tail had ripped through the back of her underwear. She knew she would be quite a sight when she changed back to a human in the morning.

If she lived long enough to change back...

A low, rumbling squeak mixed with Finigan's howls. Walter had joined the chase! "Watch yourself!" Pomona Mona called. "The dirty rat's got a gun!"

Bigfish looked back and now saw a dog, a former roller-derby star and a giant mouse pursuing him. He fired another wild shot, but they kept gaining.

Okay, he decided. I'll slow down, take careful aim and pick you off one at a time. The moon had come out from behind the clouds, and he could see them clearly as they closed on him. The crazy old woman on the skates goes first, he decided.

But as he turned to take aim, his other foot slipped off Mishka's neck. Just as he squeezed the trigger, Mishka swiveled her head and bit him on the leg as hard as she could!

"Aaaauugh!" he yelled, and his shot almost missed. Almost, but not quite.

Pomona Mona staggered, but kept coming. Bigfish kicked at Mishka with his other foot. Mishka dodged and then jumped from the cart. Bigfish tried to steady himself for another shot, but before he could fire, Walter hurtled out of the light and blindsided him. Then Finigan leaped into the cart and bit Bigfish's other leg.

Bigfish yelled with rage and pain and tried to steady himself to fire. Before he could, Pomona Mona was on him swinging the bat with all her remaining strength. The gun flew into the darkness and Bigfish collapsed with a groan.

"You broke my wrist!" he whined.

"That's not all I'm gonna break, you rat-with-a-mouse!" she said. Then a police car screeched to a stop and Officer Mulholand jumped out.

"That's enough, Mona Honey!" he commanded. "We'll take it from here. Nobody gets away from Officer Herbert J. Mulholand! And I guess he knows by now that you don't mess around with Pomona Mona either!"

"What took ya so long?" Pomona Mona asked as she wobbled a bit and dropped the bat.

"Got here as fast as we could," Mulholand said. "Is everybody all right?"

"No, as a matter of fact," Pomona Mona said. She looked at the blood running down her side and added, "I think the dirty skunk shot me!"

She took two tottering steps toward Mulholand and then fainted dead away. Mulholand caught her just before she hit the ground.

CHAPTER FOURTEEN

Leaving Home

Pomona Mona was stuck in the hospital for nearly two days. The bullet had broken a couple of ribs, and she had lost quite a bit of blood. They finally let her out when she promised to stay off her skates for a week and not chase any more armed fugitives.

The sore ribs didn't stop her from grabbing Mishka up in a big hug as soon as she got home. Mishka didn't hug her back, not wanting to hurt her, but she kissed her aunt on the cheek.

Kissing was another strange thing that humans did, but it seemed fun. She made up her mind to try it with Walter as soon as she could. Mice never kissed. It was definitely more fun being human.

"Notice anything, Honey?" Pomona Mona asked as she waved her hand in Mishka's face.

"You've got a new ring on your finger," Mishka said. "It sparkles like a..." The realization hit her suddenly. This was another unusual human custom. "Does that mean that you and Officer Mulholand are going to be... mates?"

"Yep! He'll be your Uncle Herbert pretty soon. We're gonna go through life eatin' chili dogs and whackin' bad guys together!"

Mulholand, who had been standing quietly in the background, blushed. Ivon looked closely at the ring and asked him, "Where did you get it? I need to buy one myself."

"For Cindy?" Walter asked.

"Yes, but don't tell her," Ivon said. "Right now she is minding the *sladkarnitsa* for me. I want it to be a surprise."

"That's *two* matings," said Mishka. She looked at Walter as if expecting him to say something.

"Uh, not for a while yet!" Walter said quickly. "You need to finish school, and I'm going to go back and finish too. We might even go on to college together."

"Going to college? Is that like taking a trip?"

"It is, I'm afraid," said a voice from the doorway. Agent Phipps of the FBI walked in. Shawana, Mio and Acey were with him. "We're going to have to relocate both of you."

"What?" Pomona Mona cried. "Take away my little niece? After I promised poor John on his deathbed that I'd look after her?"

"Mona, Honey," Mulholand said gently. "John Malone never existed, remember?"

"Doesn't matter!" Pomona Mona sniffed. "If he had, I sure would have promised him."

"It does matter, I'm afraid," Phipps said. "I've just come from the hospital. Mr. Ice is going to live, and he's singing like an off-key canary."

"This is all very peculiar," Mishka said once again. "Why would he want to sound like a bird?"

"Figure of speech," said Phipps. "He wants to get a lighter sentence for himself, so he's spilling everything he knows about Bigfish and his operation. I'll bet we can even get Bigfish to roll over on *his* boss!"

Mishka gave him a puzzled look and Phipps quickly added, "Another figure of speech."

"There is no honor among thieves," Mulholand explained.

"Yes," Ivon agreed. In Bulgarian we would say *Nyama chestni moshenitsi*, there are no honest rascals."

"But why do we have to leave if they are all going to jail?" Mishka asked.

"Because they are just one part of a very big, very dirty business," Phipps replied. "It's called a cartel. All the bad guys in the other parts of it are scared now, and they want to get rid of you, permanently. But we'll hide the both of you where they can never get at you."

Mishka wondered silently if this was really possible.

"What am I gonna do without my little niece to look after?" Pomona Mona sobbed.

"You and Mulholand can be foster parents," Phipps told her. "There are all kinds of boys and girls out there who need the love and care you two can provide."

Pomona Mona brightened a bit at this, but Mishka asked, "What about my friends? They need me on the team!"

"You're ineligible," Acey said sadly. "The School Activities Association just passed a rule that only full-time humans can play school sports in this state."

"It was kind of unfair," Mio admitted. "You were, well, a little *too* good."

The door flew open and Calamity Chris charged into the room. "Let's see the sparkler, Mona!" she demanded. Fortunately, she knew about the injured ribs, so she punched her friend on the arm instead of hugging her.

"Wow!" she exclaimed. "We'll get some of the girls from the old circuit together for bridesmaids! We can all wear our old uniforms, if we can still get into 'em, that is, and skate you down the aisle! Can you skate too?" she asked Officer Mulholand.

"Afraid not," Mulholand admitted.

"Too bad!" Calamity Chris said. "But Mishka, Honey, I've got great news for you. They showed your highlights on ESPN! I've got calls from 26 different colleges and universities; they all want you! And the Lakers, the Clippers, the Pacers and the Trailblazers all want to know when you'll be eligible for the NBA draft!"

"Not while she's a protected witness!" Phipps said. "You and Walter are going to have to be two very normal teenagers, if there is such a thing, for the next year or two. We're going to have to get you both new names too."

"I was just getting used to Mishka Malone," Mishka said. She sat and thought for a few minutes. "Okay, I want Marinova for my last name. That was my mother's maiden name. I don't care if she existed or not, she was my mother! That's the way I think of her! And Aunt Mona, I want to use your name too!"

"You want to be Mona Marinova?" Pomona Mona asked. "Oh, Honey, of course you can be!" And, sore ribs and all, she grabbed Mishka up in a bear hug and danced her around the room.

"This is all so odd!" Mishka said again.

"And if I'm going to have a new name," Walter said, "then I want to be Ivon Mulholand!"

Officer Mulholand beamed, but Ivon blushed.

"I must confess something," he said. "Ivon in Bulgarian is really a girl's name. My real name is Ivan. I wrote it in English as Ivon because the o reminded me of a bagel!"

"Ivan translates as John," Phipps said. "How about John Mulholand?"

"John Mulholand it is," Walter said. "I'm glad to meet you, Miss Mona Marinova!" And he put an arm around Mishka and kissed her. Mishka smiled.

"About time!" she said. Kissing was definitely nice. Humans really did have a lot more fun than mice.

"Just wait!" Acey said. "It gets even better."

"How would *you* know, Girl?" Shawana demanded, and this time Acey blushed. I wonder if I can blush too, Mishka thought. I'll have to practice.

"We came over because we want our picture taken with you before you go," Mio said.

"Sure," Mishka said, "but can't we do it at school tomorrow?"

"No," Acey said. "We want two pictures, before and after."

"She means before and after midnight," Shawana put in. "We brought our uniforms over."

Mishka shook her head. "Mice and basketball uniforms don't go together very well," she said.

"We made up a special one for you, Girl," Shawana said. "Here, have a look!"

She pulled a jersey from her backpack. It looked like Mishka's and had her number: 13. But the name had been altered. Instead of "Wildcats" it now read "Wildmice."

"I like it!" Mishka said. "But the shorts are a problem."

"You mean with your tail?" Mio asked. "We sort of, uh, modified them for you." She held them up and pointed to a long rip in the back. "That should make things more comfortable."

"Hoo-eee, man!" Shawana added. "Don't think I'd like to take the court wearing those!"

"I see what you mean," Mishka said. "I hope you folks don't mind if I don't model these before midnight!"

"When is she gonna have to leave?" Pomona Mona asked.

"We can wait until after Christmas," Phipps replied. "It will take a while to get all the paperwork done. You have never celebrated Christmas before, have you?" he asked Mishka.

"Not if it only comes once a year," she said. "Last year at this time I wasn't even born!"

"You'll like it," Phipps said, "and we'll all do our best to see that you have many, many more."

As the girls trooped upstairs to change, Mishka thought about what Phipps had said. Many, many more years. She could understand that now. She was thinking like a human more and more.

She was acting more like a human too. She had stood up to Bigfish and told him no. She had even attacked him to help save her Aunt Mona. She had friends and loved ones now, and she understood what the words meant.

But soon she would have to leave most of them.

Walter was also thinking as he walked back to the *sladkarnitsa* with Ivon. Transforming in front of people, especially girls, embarrassed him. He remembered what the old woman had told him: "From now on, your life will never be boring!" What adventures would the next few months bring?

The girls came back down with Mishka in her regular uniform, and Pomona Mona snapped a couple of pictures. Then, as midnight drew near, they went back up to wait for the transformation.

"Does it hurt?" Mio asked.

"No," Mishka said. "It feels funny, like a weight pressing down. Then it rolls past like a wave, and I'm a mouse."

"Don't think I'd like to try it, Girl!" Shawana said.

Mishka peeled off her regular uniform and waited for the transformation. Then it came. The other girls flinched a little, but they didn't scream or run. They even helped her put on the special uniform.

That's what it means to be a friend, Mishka realized. They are the ones who accept you whoever you are and however you look. She looked at her three teammates and wished that she could tell them what was going through her mind and how much they meant to her.

Three girls — black, white and Asian — all willing to work, play and share themselves with her.

Humans were very strange indeed. They could be terribly cruel, but they could be warm and caring too.

Mio seemed to guess what she was thinking. "C'mon Mishka," she said. "Let's go get that picture taken."

They ran back downstairs together. Pomona Mona was waiting with the camera. "You get in the back, you're tallest," she said to Acey. "Shawana and Mio get beside her. Everybody give a big smile!"

Mishka felt the others' arms around her. She wanted to hug them all back, but that would have to wait until morning. So instead she looked straight at the camera and tried her best to smile.

"That's great! Hold it!" Pomona Mona said, and the camera clicked.

Ending a Diary

The girl chewed on the stub of a pencil and tried to think of what to write. Writing was easier now, and her teeth didn't grow as fast as they once did. So she broke fewer pencils and didn't chew up nearly as many empty toilet paper rolls.

"Dear Aunt Mona..." she began.

But how could she set down all the things that jumbled up in her mind? There was the wonder of growing up, of learning and remembering things, of seeing new places, and the simple joy of going to sleep at night knowing she was safe.

She thought for a bit and then began to write.

So many things have happened to me over the past few months that it will take years to sort them all out. But it's wonderful to know that I *will* have years to sort them out. I can wake up in the morning and know I will not go hungry. I can walk outside in the sunshine and know that a predator will not eat me. I can be with others and we will share things and not fight over them. I like being human!

Walter and I are doing fine in school. We've kept our low profiles and done nothing unusual, but this has been hard. Yesterday we watched the track team practice. After they had left, we went over to where they had been high jumping and tried it. I cleared seven feet pretty easily; that was as high as the bar would go. That's two feet over my head, and Walter says that's pretty good. He also did it, but it took him three tries.

We are both getting straight A's. They want to send us on to college to learn more things. Humans have to spend a long time learning things, much longer than mice. But it's a lot better than being at the bottom of the food chain and winding up as some cat's dinner.

I'm giving my diary to an FBI man, who will give it to Agent Phipps, who will get it to you. I want you to have it to remember me by. And remember that I will always be,

Your loving niece,

Mishka Mona Marinova Malone

Acknowledgments

I want to express my thanks to Duncan and Barbara Dashney, computer aces both, for all their help. Thanks also to Eugenia Marinova of the World Bank, and formerly of the Bulgarian Embassy, for her translating work and for allowing me to graft Mishka onto her family tree.

Also a special thanks to the late Pat Olson, editor, linguist and scholar, who informed me one day that the opposite of a weremouse would not be a werehuman, but rather a mousewere.